"So was I right?" Penny whispered after the new boy was out of hearing range. "A real hunk, huh?"

"Yeah, he's pretty cute," Sarah agreed nonchalantly, unwilling to reveal more interest. She watched Bernard set down his tray at a small, empty table. A lock of hair fell over his eyes, giving him a shy appeal that aroused her curiosity.

Suddenly, he whipped his hair off his face with a quick swipe of his hand and, in the process, looked straight at Sarah. Embarrassed by the momentary contact, Sarah looked down and blushed. She could feel her heart beat faster.

Dear Reader,

At Silhouette we publish books with you in mind. We're pleased to announce the creation of Silhouette First Love, a new line of contemporary romances written by the finest young-adult writers as well as outstanding new authors in this field.

Silhouette First Love captures many of the same elements enjoyed by Silhouette Romance readers—love stories, happy endings and the same attention to detail and description. But First Love features young heroines and heroes in contemporary and recognizable situations.

You play an important part in our future plans for First Love. We welcome any suggestions or comments on our books and I invite you to write to us at the address below.

Karen Solem
Editor-in-Chief
Silhouette Books
P.O. Box 769
New York, N.Y. 10019

SERENADE
Adrienne Marceau

First Love from Silhouette
Published by Silhouette Books New York
America's Publisher of Contemporary Romance

SILHOUETTE BOOKS, a Simon & Schuster Division of
GULF & WESTERN CORPORATION
1230 Avenue of the Americas, New York, N.Y. 10020

ISBN: 0-671-53304-5

First Silhouette Books printing October, 1981

10 9 8 7 6 5 4 3 2 1

1

Penny Myers stood at the Jordans' front door and rang the doorbell, then turned around and surveyed the morning sunlight glistening on the dewy lawn. *It's going to be warm today,* she thought, *a great late-summer day. A beach day maybe. Certainly not a day to start school.* Penny let out a slow, resigned sigh, forcing herself to accept the fact that it really was September and today was really the first day of her senior year at Maplewood High.

"Well, good morning, Penny," the front door suddenly swung open. It was Mrs. Jordan.

"Huh? Oh, hi, Mrs. Jordan. I was just day-dreaming."

"Wishing it were the beginning of the summer again, I'll bet."

"Yeah," she signed dreamily. "Is Sarah ready to face the music?"

"Not quite. Come on in. She'll be right down."

Penny followed Sarah's mother into the kitchen. As she passed the big hallway mirror, she glared at herself, focusing on her numerous freckles and her frizzy red hair. Pausing for a split second, she frowned at her appearance and pulled at her frustrating hair in the mirror.

"Have you had breakfast, Penny?" Mrs. Jordan asked as she refilled her coffee cup. "How about a bran muffin? I just made them."

"Thanks, Mrs. Jordan, but don't tempt me. I've got to watch my weight."

"Why, Penny?" Mrs. Jordan raised her eyebrows and chuckled. "You look fine to me."

"Yeah, now I'm okay, but it's later that I'm worried about. You know, between the greasy stuff they serve at the cafeteria and the Halloween candy, and then Thanksgiving dinner, then Christmas and Easter . . . why, I could be a blimp by the time the senior prom rolls around. That's why I'm watching out now."

"I see." Mrs. Jordan nodded knowingly. "It's the prom that's on your mind."

"Yup. I never thought ole super-cool me would get all excited about being a senior, but I really am. There's a lot happening this year—new senior privileges, the prom, the Winter Carnival, graduation, college applications. It kills me to admit it, but I guess I'm really looking forward to this year."

"I'm glad to hear you say that, Penny. Now if you could only transfer a little of your enthusiasm to Sarah."

"Pining over Steve?"

Mrs. Jordan shut her eyes and just nodded demonstrably.

"But he's only been gone a week."

"I know that. But she really misses him," she whispered so Sarah wouldn't hear.

"Yeah, well, they were pretty tight," Penny confirmed. "But now that he's away at college, who knows what'll happen? He could turn into a real wild and crazy guy. If you know what I mean, Mrs. Jordan." Penny blushed, embarrassed at her spontaneous Steve Martin imitation.

Mrs. Jordan laughed. "I think I do know what you mean. But he's not that kind of guy, is he? I've always found him very considerate."

"Yeah, Steve is a pretty nice guy," Penny agreed. She decided that perhaps she shouldn't comment any further on Steve. After all, Sarah was her best friend and it just didn't seem right to be discussing Sarah's problems with her mother—even if Mrs. Jordan did mean well. "What's taking Sarah so long?" Penny quickly changed the subject. "We're going to be late if she doesn't get down here soon."

But before Mrs. Jordan could reply, Sarah shuffled sleepily into the kitchen. Sarah was slender, about 5′5″, and usually energetic, but today she seemed to be dragging a ball and chain behind her. Her normally bright hazel eyes were only half-open.

She started to say good-morning, but a voracious yawn overcame her. "Excuse me," she said, her hand over her mouth. "Good morning."

"Boy, do you ever look like a house on fire," Penny quipped. "Your basic model Maplewood High senior."

"Very funny," Sarah growled. "Don't give me a hard time. I didn't sleep well."

"First-day-back jitters?" Penny grinned knowingly.

"Hmmm? . . . yeah," Sarah murmured distractedly.

"How about a muffin, Sarah? You've got time."

"No thanks, Mom. I'm not hungry. Anyway we want to get to school early. There's always a lot of good gossip on the first day of school, and *Penny* doesn't want to miss any of it." Sarah shot her friend a sly glance.

"Me! Who do you think I am? Rona Barrett? Everyone knows my one goal at Maplewood High is the quest of knowledge." Penny stood up and put her hand over her suddenly serious-looking eyes, like Columbus searching for the New World.

"Ha!" Sarah scoffed.

"You know, I'd think you girls would want to dress up a little for the first day of school. Couldn't you bring yourselves to part with your old jeans for just one day?"

Sarah and Penny regarded each other incredulously. Penny was wearing a plum-colored French T-shirt and her old Adidas with her faded Levi's. The color of her T-shirt went well with her unruly

8

red hair, she thought. Sarah was wearing her favorite shirt, the red and white gingham-check western shirt with the mother-of-pearl snap buttons, her tan moccasins, and her newest pair of designer jeans. With her shoulder-length chestnut hair fixed in one thick braid down her back, she was positive that she looked very cowboy and quite stylish.

"But these are practically brand-new jeans, Mom."

"And this is a new top, Mrs. Jordan. This is actually the first time I'm wearing it!"

"Yes, but you look as though you're going to the gym. A good pair of slacks and a nice blouse seems more appropriate for the first day of school, don't you think?"

"But then we'd look like . . . like the teachers, Mrs. Jordan." Penny squinted, trying to understand Mrs. Jordan's complaint.

"I'm sorry I brought it up." Mrs. Jordan laughed, shaking her head. "I don't know what got into me. Must be getting old, I guess."

Sarah smiled at her mother's ability to laugh at herself. Of course, she was kidding about "getting old" because she was generally considered the most with-it and easiest-to-talk-to of all her friends' parents.

"Well, it's too late for you two young belles to get into your crinolines and hoop skirts, so I guess you'll just have to make do with your jeans."

"Yeah. I guess so, Mom." Sarah giggled.

"Now go forth and soak up some knowledge. And

Sarah," Mrs. Jordan continued as she saw them out the door, "please eat something for lunch. I don't want you missing meals."

"Okay, Mom. I promise."

"Your mother's great, Sarah," Penny commented after Mrs. Jordan closed the door behind them and they had started down the front steps.

"Yeah. . . ." Sarah's attention suddenly started to drift away.

"Ground Control to Sarah Jordan. Come in, Jordan. Are you there, Sarah?" Penny mimicked. She had a pretty good idea what was on her friend's mind.

"Oh . . . yeah. I'm just a little tired." Sarah wasn't listening very intently. Her mind was somewhere else.

"Come on, Sarah. Snap out of it," Penny said, stopping in her tracks and pushing the nagging stray strands of hair out of her face in annoyance. "I know what's bothering you, but pining away for Steve won't bring him back from college."

Sarah stopped and glared at her friend angrily. "My relationship with Steve is none of your—" Suddenly she stopped, her fury quickly burning out. "I'm sorry, Penny. I didn't mean to yell at you. It's just . . . it's just that I miss him and . . . I haven't heard from him in over a week." A big tear rolled down her cheek. She tried to brush it away before Penny noticed.

Penny just looked at her, wishing she could adequately express the sympathy she felt for her best friend. "I . . . I just don't know what to say. I know it must be rough for you now, but it's just something you'll have to get used to. I mean, you wouldn't want him to quit college just to come back here to be with you."

"Of course not. Remember, he wanted to go to NYU and commute from home just so we could stay together. But when he got into Cornell, I was the one who told him he'd be stupid if he didn't go. I'm really glad that he got in, I want him to be there. I just wish I didn't feel the way I do. So . . . alone and empty."

"Look, Sarah, this is our senior year. We're finally the big kids. We're supposed to be living it up, right?"

"You live it up for both of us. I don't feel like it."

"No, seriously. We've got a lot to look forward to. The football games, college applications, graduation, parties, the Winter Carnival, the prom—"

"Yeah. Do you think they'll let me go to the prom alone? Do you think Steve will be able to take time out from his classes just to take me to the Winter Carnival Ball?" Fresh tears welled up in her eyes.

"Sarah Jordan, you better stop crying right now!" Penny angrily thrust the flyaway wisps of hair off her face, startling Sarah. "I feel for you—you know I do. But it's no good feeling sorry for yourself. You're just going to make yourself miserable. And if you're miserable, I'm miserable. Do you want to blow my senior year? Of course you don't. So let's get going before we're late." Penny locked her arm through Sarah's and started to escort her down the block.

Sarah smiled weakly and turned to her determined friend. "You're right. Moping around like this is ridiculous. I'm sorry I acted so terribly. I promise to shape up. Really. I don't want to get a reputation for being a dishrag. I promise to have fun this year—if it kills me."

But as they approached the familiar red-brick facade of the high school, Sarah felt a renewed pang of longing for Steve. The front steps where they had often hung out, the balding stretch of lawn where he liked to play Frisbee with his buddies, even the old statue of the Civil War veteran that Steve and his friends wrapped up in gauze last Halloween so that it looked like a mummy—everything she saw reminded her of Steve Dowd. The butterflies returned to her stomach and her legs began to stiffen. The thought of entering that building and starting her senior year without Steve suddenly made her panic. She bit her lip and clenched onto Penny's arm for support.

Penny, however, eager to hear the latest gossip, did not realize what was happening to her friend and dragged her along as she dove into the crowd.

"Sarah, look! There's Bob Hersh, the captain of the football team. Will you look at his head! A crew cut! Geez, what a jerk!"

"Yeah. . . ." Sarah timidly glanced from face to face in the crowd, but she mainly concentrated on Penny, trying to monopolize her so she wouldn't be left alone.

"I don't believe it! Sarah, don't look now, but Jean Marks dyed her hair *jet black!* No, don't look now. Be cool. It's all spiky and punk. And—she's turning toward us—oh, wow! Her eyes are all lined in black and her lips are blood red. Wait'll Mrs. Graham sees this. She'll send her home for sure."

But Jean Marks' new punk look didn't interest Sarah either. Now she wished they hadn't come so early after all. Although she couldn't exactly say why, she felt very uncomfortable around the people she had spent three years with at Maplewood High, and she was ashamed to feel the way she did. Without Steve, she felt naked and incomplete.

But I'm an individual, she told herself, I can function on my own. But she and Steve had been *the* Maplewood High item. And they were somewhat of a school legend, having been together—glued together was more like it—since the end of her freshman year. People said they had gone steady longer than any other couple at Maplewood High—ever! The kids at school seldom mentioned one without mentioning the other. Most of the other girls in school envied her for her solid relationship. Even though she had never flaunted her boyfriend and often encouraged her friends when they didn't have dates, it was clear that a certain few girls in her class really hated her. Now that she was without Steve, these girls probably couldn't wait to gloat over her loss, and Sarah was dreading the thought of the taunts and mean teasing she would have to endure from those few envious seniors.

"Hey, Sarah, get a load of this," Penny broke into her anxious daydream.

Sarah turned and looked where Penny indicated. Standing out prominently amidst her clique of followers was Lisa Forster, the "queen of the preppy girls," as Penny called her. Sarah instantly felt ill. Lisa Forster was unquestionably at the top of the list of the jealous girls whom Sarah didn't want to confront.

"Well if it isn't Little Miss Hotsy-Totsy," Penny said in a singsong voice, gyrating her shoulders to emphasize her words. "She denies it, but I swear those golden tresses get a shade lighter every season. And that outfit—she looks like she's going to the country club."

Lisa was certainly overdressed in comparison to the other students gathering around the front steps of the high school. While almost everyone wore jeans or cords, Lisa wore a bright kelly green wraparound skirt with matching espadrilles and a pink broadcloth, button-down shirt with the sleeves turned up halfway to her elbow. And even though the temperature would surely reach the eighties today, Lisa wore a baby-girl pink cotton sweater draped over her shoulders with the sleeves loosely tied around her front. Her long straight hair was pulled back in a high ponytail tied with a piece of thick green yarn, and her bangs were carefully feathered to flop correctly on either side of her meticulously mascaraed upper and lower eyelashes. From where they were standing, Sarah and Penny could see that she had a pack of cigarettes half-inserted and prominently displayed in the side pouch of her leather bag.

"Oh, oh, she's seen us," Penny murmured sarcastically out of the side of her mouth. "The queen is going to bless us with her presence. I think I'll faint."

Sarah wanted to die on the spot as Lisa fixed her gaze upon her and casually sauntered over to them.

"Hi, Sarah, Penny," Lisa oozed. "Have a good summer?"

"Can't complain," Penny blurted out.

"Yeah," Sarah managed, her throat constricting.

"Great. What did you do?" Lisa's enthusiasm was obviously put-on.

"Went to the shore a lot," Penny offered boldly. "And to see Springsteen at the Garden."

"Oh . . . nice. How about you, Sarah?"

"Oh, nothing exciting"—she cleared her throat nervously—"couple of weeks in Nova Scotia with my family."

"Sounds *super*. Well, *I* worked most of the summer. For my uncle's newspaper on the Cape."

"The Cape?" Penny questioned.

"Cape *Cod*, Penny. You've heard of it, haven't you?"

"Vaguely."

"Well, anyway, I was sort of a junior reporter for the *South Dennis Gazette*. Really a lot of work. But I did manage to make it to the beach as often as I could." Lisa pouted slightly as if she were regretting all the sunny days she missed, slaving over her typewriter in the office. The depth of her tan, however, indicated otherwise.

Sarah wished the school bell would ring so she could flee to class. It was clear that Lisa was just warming up.

"By the way, Sarah," she continued, craning her neck to look behind Sarah and Penny, "where's Steve?"

Sarah turned gray. *Here it comes,* she thought.

"I knew something was missing. Sarah without Steve is like . . . well, strawberries without cream."

"Oh, man—" Penny moaned to herself.

"Steve's at college," Sarah spoke up shakily.

"Oh, that's right. He graduated *last* year. I guess I always assumed he was in our class because you two were always together."

Hearing Lisa say "were" pierced Sarah's heart. Why didn't that stupid bell ring?

"He's at Rutgers, right?"

"No. Cornell."

"Cornell! Really? That's where my father went."

"What a coincidence," Penny breathed.

"He's really lucky. You know, Cornell is right up there. Behind Harvard, Yale and Columbia."

"That's where my brother goes—Columbia," Sarah offered, trying to sidetrack the conversation.

"Oh. . . ." Lisa was disinterested. "Good for Steve, though. But *too* bad for you, Sarah. I mean senior year and all, and Steve has to go away to Cornell. Poor baby, I really feel *awful* for you."

Sarah began to feel the tears welling in her eyes again when the school bell finally rang out. *Thank heavens,* she thought. But she knew the relief was only temporary.

"Bye-ee," Lisa chirped. "See you two around." And she bounded off at a half-trot with her ponytail bouncing behind her like a snippy poodle's tail.

"I'll meet you in the cafeteria at lunch," Penny jabbered, about to dash off to her first class. "You've got fifth period lunch, right?"

"Ah, yeah . . . fifth period . . . see you later." Feeling washed-out and very unsure of herself, Sarah climbed the front steps very slowly. She was the last student to enter the front doors of Maplewood High.

2

Sarah took a tray from the stack at the end of the lunch line and grabbed some plastic silverware and a paper napkin. She still wasn't very hungry, but since she had promised her mother that she'd eat lunch, she thought she might as well go through the line and see if anything appealed to her.

A blast of salty steam with an unidentifiable odor came from behind the glass partition quickly reminding Sarah that nothing was ever appealing at the cafeteria. She pushed her tray along the metal rails, lethargically surveying the offerings. Meat loaf and hot turkey sandwiches. *Yuk!* The boy ahead of her ordered the meat loaf, and the woman behind the counter generously ladled lumpy brown gravy all over the slab of meat and the mashed potatoes.

"Next," the woman warbled.

Sarah just shook her head. "No thanks," she murmured and passed down the line. Maybe the sandwiches were better.

The hot sandwiches didn't look any more appetizing than the meat loaf. Enormous meatballs balanced inside even bigger rolls with tomato sauce dumped all over. Sarah moved on.

Next came the huge tray of french fries doled out by Sam, the friendly old guy who, it seemed, had worked in that kitchen forever.

"Welcome back to school," Sam beamed at Sarah. "How about some fries?"

Sarah smiled, then stared down at the mass of greasy french fries. *Each one is a new zit,* she thought. "Ah . . . not today, Sam, thanks."

She proceeded to the desserts and salads, but the array of semismashed pies and heavily frosted cakes did not look too appetizing. The bright green Jell-O looked like blocks of Day-Glo plastic. She looked ahead in the line, but the only things left were the Twinkies, Devil Dogs and Suzie-Qs, and then the beverages. Blah!

But just then she spotted a lone scoop of tuna salad sitting on a bed of not-too-terrible-looking lettuce. *That's it,* she thought and quickly snatched it from between the rows of Jell-O and fruit salad. After fixing herself some plain tea in a Styrofoam cup, she paid the cashier and gladly left the lunch line.

The lunch room was just as she remembered it—chaos. The old cliques were seated at their usual tables, talking a mile a minute, laughing too loud, fooling around. The boys from the chess club held their old table, playing chess in spite of all the noise. Sarah was amazed that anyone could concentrate here. Then as she stood with her tray, surveying the room for a place to sit, it suddenly occurred to her that she had no special place because she didn't belong to any of these groups. She had always had lunch with Steve and his friends. But now that they had all graduated, she was the only one left. Penny was practically her only friend from her own class. Unable to spot Penny in the crowd, Sarah skulked over to an empty table full of trays, empty cups with bent straws and dirty plates. She sighed as she cleared away a place for herself and started to pick at her tuna salad.

Just three more periods to go, she thought as she looked over her schedule card. *English, then homeroom, then American History, then home.* She smiled when she looked at "Am. Hist." written into the eighth period box on her schedule. Ms. Stillman was teaching American History II, and she was by far the most popular teacher at Maplewood High. Sarah had had her last year for American History I, and they had gotten along fantastically. Sarah knew that Ms. Stillman liked her because she would occasionally defer to Sarah in class, knowing that Sarah was something of a history buff. And, of course, Sarah could never really dislike any teacher who gave her an A for the year.

She continued to examine her schedule, assessing her classes and comparing her teachers. Unfortunately, compared to Ms. Stillman, the others were pretty ordinary, if not plain awful.

For English she had old Miss Edwards. Steve had had her last year, and he always complained about how boring her lectures were. "Wait'll she makes you read *The Faerie Queene*—you'll want to lie down and die!" he warned.

Mr. Shapiro taught advanced math. He was a pretty good guy—always gave makeup tests, Steve said. Obviously very bright, but his jokes were the worst, according to Steve and his buddies.

"Chrome-Dome" for Economics, good ole Mr. Rizzo with his shiny round head. Everyone said he was a real pain, but since the alternative was Physics, Sarah was willing to put up with anything. After Chemistry, she didn't want to go near another science class.

French III was with Mme. O'Rourke, naturally. The Julia Child of Maplewood High, Steve once said.

Gym? She wasn't sure who she'd get this year. Last year Steve had Mr. Conway, but—

Sarah suddenly stopped and shoved her schedule card into her notebook. Why does everything have to relate back to Steve? Why can't I stop thinking about him for just a little while? she asked herself.

The blob of tuna salad sat before her like an old, fuzzy tennis ball left out in the rain too long. She was staring at it gloomily when Penny showed up.

"Hey! What're you doing over here? We never used to sit over here, Sarah. I've been eating with

Laura and Mike—guess we didn't see each other.
Come on over. Mike is telling us about his trip out
West, riding the rapids and all." Penny was clearly
excited to be back at school, but she wished she
could share some of her spirit with poor Sarah.
"Come on, Sarah. This table is filthy anyway."

"Ah . . . no thanks, Penny. I'm almost finished
and—"

"Sarah, are you going to snap out of it or what?"
Penny scowled with her hands on her hips and her
brow furrowed.

Sarah looked up at her friend. "I will snap out of
it, I promise. I just need a little time to adjust. That's
all. Sit down, Pen, and tell me the latest gossip.
Maybe that'll help me ease back into things. Okay?"

Penny frowned and sighed, "Okay."

"So how are your classes? You had gym this
morning? Who did you get?"

"The new gym teacher, Mrs. Stanton. They say
she was in the army, and she looks pretty tough. She
was pretty nice today, though. But I guess everyone's nice on the first day of school."

"Yeah. How about English? How's Miss Edwards?"

"Oh, spare me, please." Penny threw up her
hands. "That woman hasn't changed since Alaska
became a state. A class with her is like warm milk.
She started right in on 'the importance of being able
to construct a clear and concise term paper' and the
'all-important first step—research.'" Penny mimicked Miss Edwards's thin, spacy voice. "Do you
know that she wants us to go out and get three-by-

five file cards—no other size will do—for the research notes? I mean, what's wrong with plain old notebook paper?"

"She's a real character. Steve always said . . ." Sarah let her sentence trail off, deciding that she shouldn't talk about him so much.

"Hey," Penny went on, ignoring Sarah's reference to Steve, "is the new boy in any of your classes?"

"What new boy?"

"There's a new senior in school. I think he's French. His name is Bernard something and he's in my math class, and is he ever cute. Very continental, you can tell just by looking at him."

"Yeah? What does he look like?"

"Well, he's not real tall, but he looks like he's got muscles and a big chest."

Sarah winced.

"Well, I don't mean he's the Hulk! Well-proportioned is what I mean. I bet he looks really good in a bathing suit."

"Okay, what else?"

"He's got big, intelligent-looking eyes that look a little sad sometimes. I couldn't tell what color from where I was sitting, though. And sandy brown hair, straight and longish—but not real long. You know?"

"Go on," Sarah prompted, enjoying Penny's rapturous description.

"And he has a very intelligent face. Very serious but sensitive-looking."

Sarah giggled. "How can you tell if someone's sensitive by his face? Attila the Hun could have been 'sensitive-looking.' "

"Go ahead and laugh"—Penny turned up her nose—"see if I care. But I'm certainly not the only one who thinks he's a hunk."

"Who else?"

"Practically every girl in class who's seen him. Including Lisa."

"You don't mean super-cool Lisa Forster, cub reporter?"

"None other than."

"Did she promise to interview him for her uncle's newspaper? Then did he promise to take her away to the Casbah?" Sarah chortled at the thought of frosty Lisa Forster acting like some sultry romantic leading lady.

"She wished," Penny declared. "I watched her try to sink her claws into him, but he politely backed away. He seems kind of shy."

"What do you think she'll—"

"Look, there he is," Penny interrupted. "He's at the cashier now."

Sarah turned to check out this new heartthrob.

Standing with his lunch tray, looking for an empty table was Bernard. To Sarah's surprise, Penny was right. He was cute. But not in a sweet way. Bernard seemed to be much more mature than the other senior boys. Sarah wondered if he might be somewhat older. His European background was evident in the clothes he wore, a tailored blue blazer over a pale blue, open collar shirt and cream-colored dress slacks. Sarah wondered if he even owned a pair of jeans. As he passed close to their table, both Penny and Sarah looked away, not wanting him to see their interest.

"So was I right?" Penny whispered after the new boy was out of hearing range. "A real hunk, huh?"

"Yeah, he's pretty cute," Sarah agreed nonchalantly, unwilling to reveal more than the mildest interest in another boy. She glanced past Penny and saw Bernard setting down his tray at a small, empty table. His hair had fallen over his eyes, making him look more boyish. Sarah decided that he probably wasn't much older than seventeen, eighteen at the most. Suddenly he whipped the hair off his face with a quick swipe of his hand, and in the process he looked up, straight at Sarah. Embarrassed with their momentary eye contact, Sarah glanced down and blushed. Fortunately, Penny didn't notice.

"I bet she'll launch an all-out attack on this one," Penny moaned.

"Who?"

"The preppy queen! Lisa! Who else?"

"Huh?"

"Ground Control to Sarah Jordan. Come in, Sarah." Penny held her nose to imitate the nasal sound of a radio broadcast again.

"I'm here, I'm here. Geez, what a comedian!" Sarah smirked.

"What I was saying, my dear, is that I'll bet you five dollars ole Lisa is already plotting her strategy for snagging this new guy."

"What makes you say that?"

"Just stands to reason, that's all. She broke up

with Billy O'Connor just before school let out last spring. If she had a new boyfriend, I'm sure we would have heard about it by now. Right?"

"Yeah . . ." Sarah was still skeptical.

"Well, a social butterfly like Lisa will have to have an escort for all the senior events. And knowing her, I'm sure she'd just love to have a real French beau. Be seen with the right type in all the right places, you know."

"Yeah, I guess you've got her psyched out pretty well."

"Of course, she's as easy to read as a comic book."

"So are *you* going to give her a run for her money? Sounds like you wouldn't mind going to a foreign movie with Jean-Paul."

"His name is Bernard . . . I think. And even if I do appreciate checking out a good-looking guy now and then, I'm taken."

Sarah had to laugh at Penny's righteous indignation. "Come on, Pen. You're *always* complaining about Gary."

"I am not 'always complaining about Gary'! True, he's not perfect and sometimes he can be a real pain, but you know, he's always there. At least I know he really likes me, and he does take me out a lot."

"Yeah! To Kung Fu movies and weird punk rock concerts!"

"Not all the time. I did get him to go to a couple of discos this summer. And he even danced once."

"Really? You never told me about that."

"It was while you were away with your family. It

wasn't as if he was John Travolta or anything," she admitted, looking down at the table. "In fact, he hated it so much, he said he'd never dance again. We're gonna look pretty stupid at the prom, sitting out every dance."

"Oh, don't worry about it now. Gary'll change his mind before the prom."

"Well, I hope so."

"But you still haven't answered my question. Why are you so interested in this new guy?"

"Well, actually, Sarah, I was thinking he's new and he probably doesn't have a girl friend yet. And you know, with all the senior events coming up and Steve away at Cornell, maybe you and—"

"Forget about it!" Sarah exploded. "I'm still going with Steve. Nothing has changed. He promised me he'd be back for the prom and maybe the Winter Carnival, too, if he doesn't have exams then. Look," Sarah added, seeing her friend's downcast expression, "it's nice of you to be concerned—honest, I appreciate it—but please don't try to play Cupid. Okay?"

"Okay. Sorry I even suggested—"

"No apologies, Penny. I'm not mad at you. I just want you to understand where things stand with me and Steve."

"Okay, now I understand, and I promise not to meddle. I'm going up for a coffee. You want anything?"

"No thanks." Sarah had barely touched her tuna salad and her tea was cold.

"Okay, I'll be right back."

Sarah pushed her tray away and propped her chin on her hand and stared out the window at nothing in particular. The boisterous cafeteria crowd had dwindled and now Sarah could make out the words of the song coming from the jukebox. Unconsciously she murmured the lyrics to herself. "'Don't go changin' . . .'" It was Billy Joel's "Just the Way You Are."

Outside kids were congregating in groups, horsing around, laughing. All the while Billy Joel's voice echoed through her mind. "'I love you just the way you are,'" Sarah sang softly with the record, ". . . Steve."

3

. . . Now for the next class, I want you to read chapters thirteen and fourteen. And while you're reading, I want you to consider the social, political, and economic factors in this country that led up to America's involvement in World War I." Ms. Stillman stood at the front of the room, casually leaning on her desk as she lectured. This hadn't been a typical first lecture, for Kathy Stillman was an exceptional teacher. To her history wasn't an endless series of isolated names, places and dates. All events related to one another, and all political decisions in history were influenced by other less obvious factors, which in turn always affected other events.

While Ms. Stillman spoke of the robber barons and their incredible wealth and power, Sarah Jordan's concentration was focused on the new boy's broad back. Gradually Sarah had lost track of Ms. Stillman's tales of monopolies and trusts as Bernard's profile became too alluring. After careful consideration, Sarah had concluded that Bernard had to be French royalty with that ruggedly handsome profile. *A regal nose if there ever was one,* she thought. High brow—very intelligent. And Penny was right, she mused, his shoulders are broad, must be muscular.

"Does anyone have any questions?" Ms. Stillman asked in conclusion and suddenly Sarah emerged from her fog, amazed that the lecture was already over. She blushed when she realized that she had missed most of the class because she was ogling at the new boy.

Ms. Stillman looked about the room, pushing her shoulder-length, ash blonde hair behind her ears and smoothing her skirt as she waited for someone to work up a question. At least a full minute passed and the silence became embarrassing. "My, my," she finally said. "No questions? I must have covered everything. Well, I always told my mother I was a great teacher."

The class laughed at this typical Kathy Stillman comment. She had a wry sense of humor that kept students amused and on their toes. If you didn't pay attention, you'd surely miss her more subtle comments, and if you didn't respond appropriately, it was a sure sign that you were daydreaming. Sarah vowed to herself that she would never allow herself to be embarrassed like that—not even to stare at a cute boy for forty minutes.

"Now before you people rush home for oxygen or whatever you need after your first *grueling* day back in school, I have an important announcement to make for those of you who play musical instruments."

Puzzled, the class began to buzz. What did music have to do with American History II?

"This year Maplewood High is sponsoring a Junior Professionals' Program to give students the opportunity to run their own businesses. There will be several businesses in several different fields, and each one will have a volunteer professional from the community as well as a faculty advisor. Initially the groups will be small—from fifteen to twenty students maximum. However, if a business shows a profit, it may expand in the spring and take on more students. I want to stress that only those students who are truly interested in learning how to run a business should volunteer for this program because each student will be required to take care of the business's books as well. In other words, paying whatever bills there will be for overhead, eventually earning enough to pay yourselves salaries, setting up employee benefit plans, purchasing insurance for the place of business, *and* paying taxes to the government. The school will lend each business a small amount of money for working capital to get yourselves started, but you will be expected to start making a profit soon after you open because you must pay back your loan. Also, no business will be bailed out. It will be strictly sink or swim."

A ripple of excitement spread throughout the class

as many of the seniors became intrigued by the challenge of running their own businesses.

"Now just to give you an example of what's involved here, let's take the Junior Professionals' Theater, which will be moderated by Mr. Rizzo—"

A groan of disapproval rose from the back of the room at the mention of "Chrome-Dome's" name.

"The Junior Professionals' Theater, will also have Mr. Lou Ciofi as its advisor," Ms. Stillman continued hurriedly. "Mr. Ciofi is retired now, but during his career he was a talent agent, promoter and a theater owner. He will show his group how to book talent, rent films, how to advertise, etc. But I would discourage would-be actors and film buffs from joining this group because you must remember that you are running a business first and foremost. You'll have to be able to contend with booking agents, film distributors, food and beverage merchants, perhaps the police if your crowds are large enough, the town health inspectors when you serve food, and so on. Basically what I am trying to impress upon you is that only people with some business sense or people who want to get some business sense should join these groups.

"Which brings me to the matter of the business that I will be moderating—the Junior Professionals' Music School. Yes, my tin ears and I will be helping the music school with its finances, scheduling, billing, and all the rest of the dull stuff. Meanwhile, the volunteer professional will advise the student teachers on their lessons, how to deal with their pupils, how to promote the music school, and all the fun stuff." She frowned mischievously and gazed about the room for a moment. "The volunteer professional we've lined up for the music school is also retired, a professional musician. Some of you may have heard of him, I think. His name is Jon Pearce."

Several people gasped. The class was dumb-founded. She couldn't be serious! Not *Jon Pearce!*

"I guess you've heard of him," she said over the excited chatter.

Who at Maplewood High hadn't heard of Jon Pearce? He was only the lead guitarist of the Makers, and one of the greatest rock 'n' roll bands in the world. Jon Pearce was also Maplewood High's most illustrious graduate in recent memory. Everyone at Maplewood High knew who he was and most followed his career with the Makers closely. They had had two hit singles and a hit album in the past two years, and if Maplewood High had an anthem, it had to be the Makers' first hit, "Us," featuring Jon Pearce's lightning guitar work. It was generally agreed, even outside Maplewood High, that Jon was one of the top lead guitarists in rock. He was naturally a source of great pride for the students of his alma mater, and needless to say, it came as quite a shock to the school when it was announced last spring that Jon was leaving the group. But even if he was retired from the Makers now, it was hard to believe that he would be returning to his hometown to work at the high school.

Ms. Stillman waited patiently for the uproar to die down. "I know you're all dying to know all about Jon Pearce," she finally said. "All I can tell you is that he is not permanently retired, just taking a break from the group for a while. This means we may only have him for a few months, but I think you'll agree we're pretty lucky to have him at all."

"You bet," Gary Ryan, Penny's boyfriend, exclaimed enthusiastically.

"Thank you for your approval, Gary. Now if we can get back to the music school for a moment. . . ."

The class gradually settled down.

"We want people who play musical instruments well enough to teach them. Mr. Pearce will audition everyone. Selection will be based upon what instrument you play, as well as how well you play it. Which means the music school will not be able to take as many guitarists as will no doubt audition."

A few isolated moans emerged from several mediocre guitar pickers in the room.

"Well, look on the bright side. If you can play tuba, you're probably a shoo-in." No one laughed. "Anyway, for those who are interested and want to start practicing for the audition, Mr. Pearce told me to tell you that he'd like candidates to prepare two pieces, each one in a different style. Rock and jazz, or classical and rock, or whatever, okay? There will be a general meeting for people interested in the music school this Thursday after school in Room 251. Now that's just for the music school. The other businesses and their meetings will be announced on the main bulletin board, or the faculty advisors will probably mention them in their classes. Is that clear?"

Just then the 2:45 bell rang, and the restless class

began to file out of the room, released finally from their first day of school. Sarah, however, remained in her seat thinking about Ms. Stillman's announcement about the Junior Professionals' Music School and wondering how many others would audition to be piano teachers. She had been thinking pretty seriously about business administration as a major in college next year, and this might be the perfect opportunity to see if she were really cut out for business, she thought to herself. Fingering her braid, she smiled. The more she thought about it, the better the music school sounded. Her piano playing was certainly better than average, since she'd taken lessons for seven years before she got bored with it and quit when she was in the eighth grade. A frown darkened her face as she recalled the last time she tried to plow her way through a Chopin polonaise. When she'd stopped taking lessons, she'd stopped practicing every day and started ignoring the more difficult music, so she wasn't as good as she used to be. On the other hand, she did play at least three or four times a week, and people did often compliment her on her playing. So why not? I will audition, she resolved. Gathering up her books, she started to consider what two pieces she would play for her audition.

When she finally looked up, she suddenly realized that she was the only one left in the room except for Ms. Stillman and that new boy. There were up at the front of the class, discussing something. Sarah quickly stood up and walked toward the door, not wanting Ms. Stillman to think she was hanging around because she wanted to talk to her. As she passed by them, Sarah glanced at Ms. Stillman and gave her a small wave.

"So long, Sarah. See you tomorrow," she said, interrupting her conversation with Bernard. And before Sarah turned away to leave, he looked over at her and their eyes met again. This time he averted his glance, then picked up his conversation with Ms. Stillman.

Out in the hallway, Penny, who had just come from Economics, and Gary were waiting for Sarah. Gary was talking loudly and gesturing wildly with his long, gangly arms while Penny just looked very confused.

"Sarah," Penny overrode Gary's monologue, "will you please tell me what this space-shot over here is talking about? Something about Jon Pearce, the Makers, a music school, and drums."

"Oh, the Junior Professionals' Music School?"

"I guess so," Penny said while motioning to Gary to be quiet and let Sarah talk.

"Do you know about the Junior Professionals' Program?"

"Yeah, Chrome-Dome told us all about it in class. Can you believe a grouch like that is going to work on a theater? I don't think he knows what it means to have fun."

"Yeah, we heard all about Chrome-Dome's cabaret from Ms. Stillman," Gary told her impatiently.

"Okay, so there's going to be a Junior Professionals' Music School too, where kids who play instruments will give lessons and run the school," Sarah explained. "Ms. Stillman is the moderator, and the professional advisor is—"

"—Jon Pearce, man!" Gary interrupted in his excitement. "Jon Pearce of the Makers! I can't believe it! *I can't believe it!*"

"Calm down, Godzilla," Penny scowled, "they aren't asking you to join the group."

"Aw, you don't understand, Pen. See, if I get into the music school—teaching drums, of course—then I'll get to know ole Jon and he can give me tips on how to make it big in a band! I mean, what better connection into the rock business could I get? This is a golden opportunity for me. Come on, let's go. I gotta get home to practice."

"Hey, Gary, remember what Ms. Stillman said about being interested in running a business as well as teaching music?" Sarah reminded him. "Doesn't sound like you're really into learning how to set up schedules and pay taxes and all of that."

"*Au contraire,* my dear Sarah," he raised a single bony finger, a thin smile creasing his long face, "I am *very* interested in learning about running a business. My dad's been bugging me for years that I should take some interest in his store, you know, learn the family business. See, he thinks I'm too dumb to get into college, so he figures I'll be taking over the hardware store. Little does he know that I'm really gonna be a millionaire rock star."

"Somehow I don't think this is the right attitude for the music school, Gary." Sarah shook her head.

"Hey, I'll do the business stuff, no question about it. And besides, who else in school can play drums like me? No one. When Jon Pearce hears me play, he's gonna say, 'That kid's got *talent*. We just *have* to have this Ryan kid teaching in this music school!'"

"Dream on, Gary, dream on," Penny commented sarcastically.

"Go ahead and make fun now, but you'll see."

"Ah . . . why don't you two save your squabbles for your own time, huh?"

"Sarah, we don't argue, we discuss."

"I beg to differ, Gary dear," Penny corrected, "we *argue*. Believe me, do we argue."

"All right, cut it, you two," Sarah declared, stepping between them. "Now since you're going to be a millionaire soon, Gary, how about taking us to Burger King? Suddenly I'm starved."

"Yeah, cheapskate, how about it?" Penny growled.

"What is this, an ambush? You trying to make me look cheap? Well, come on, I'll show you. Cokes all around."

"*And* burgers?" Penny demanded.

"Hmmm . . . okay, you win. Burgers, too."

Grinning with their victory, Penny and Sarah took one arm each and dragged Gary down the hall and out of the building before he could change his mind.

4

When Sarah arrived at Room 251 on Thursday after her last class, there were already about a dozen seniors there. Looking around for a seat, she spotted Gary sitting up front, beating his Economics textbook furiously with a pair of drumsticks.

"Hey, Gary! Is this something new? I thought you played drums."

"Haven't you ever heard of hitting the books, Sarah?" Gary laughed uproariously at his own joke.

"That was pretty bad, Gary, pretty bad."

"No, it was funny," he continued to chortle.

Sarah put her books down on the desk next to Gary's, then dug into her shoulder bag for an elastic band. The weather was still more like summer than fall, and Sarah was itching to brush the loose strands of hair back and off her forehead. Finding an elastic amidst the wide assortment of paraphernalia she carried around with her every day, Sarah pulled all her hair back and made a ponytail. Before finally taking her seat, she pulled her powder blue T-shirt away from the small of her back where it stuck with sweat.

"Hey, Sarah," Gary finally stopped drumming, "did you hear? Penny's going out for one of the other Junior Professionals' groups."

"Really? She didn't say anything to me."

"Yeah, that's 'cause she's been debating about it all week."

"What group did she pick?"

"You won't believe it. Chrome-Dome's cabaret! No wonder she didn't want to mention it to anyone."

"Actually, running a theater sounds as though it could be fun. And Mr. Rizzo isn't so bad once you get to know him. At least that's what I hear."

"Do my ears deceive me? Or are you just getting soft? Talking for Chrome-Dome? Come on, Sarah!"

"He's just a little . . . peculiar, that's all. You make him sound like the Creature from the Black Lagoon."

"Any guy who stands on the radiators when he's teaching isn't all there, as far as I'm concerned."

Sarah just shrugged. Sometimes it just wasn't worth discussing anything with Gary—as Penny often said to Sarah—because when his mind was made up, that was it. Unfortunately, students had been making fun of Mr. Rizzo for as long as she was at Maplewood High, and it seemed to Sarah that Gary was just mindlessly carrying on the tradition.

"Hey, Sarah," Gary quickly changed the subject, "you hear anything from Steve?"

Sarah's heart sank at the mention of Steve's name. He was a sore subject with her, and she had even snapped at her mother once over dinner when she brought up his name. It was now almost three weeks since he went away, and she hadn't even received a note from him. Of course, everyone she saw seemed to ask about him, making her feel like a Siamese twin, incomplete without the other one. She began to think that other people could see an invisible scar where the scalpel had cut them apart. Gary's asking about Steve now was just like throwing salt on her infected wound.

"Sarah?" Gary could see that her mind had drifted off somewhere else. "I said did you hear from Steve?"

"Ah . . . yeah," she lied, "he's doing fine."

"He likes it up there at Cornell?"

"Yup."

"That's great."

Then Sarah noticed the new boy, Bernard, entering the room. He was dressed more casually today in khaki pants and a maroon Lacoste tennis shirt that showed off his broad chest and muscular biceps. Nervously switching his load of books from one arm to the other, he looked around for an empty seat and went straight to the back of the room where he could sit alone. As he made his way to the back, Gary caught his eye and they exchanged tentative nods.

"Do you know him?" Sarah whispered to Gary.

"Not really. He's in my gym class."

"He's French, isn't he?"

"Belgian, I think. His name is Bernard Saint-something."

"Hmmm. . . ."

"Yeah, his locker is near mine. He seems like a nice guy, but he's very quiet. Until today, I thought he couldn't speak English. He was giving some of the guys tips on soccer. Man, you ought to see him play."

"He's in our history class, too. I've never heard him talk at all. Seems very mysterious."

"I don't know about that," Gary shrugged. "He's just a guy."

"Yeah, but you can tell he's European from his looks and his clothes. Continental, you know?"

"What's so continental? Hey, how come you're so interested in Bernard?" he asked with a sly grin.

"Well . . ." she began to blush as he put her on the spot, "well, it's just good to see a guy who dresses nicely, that's all. Look at you—old jeans and that T-shirt," she pointed at his black T-shirt with the metallic red and blue Makers logo, now cracked and peeling with age. "Looking for brownie points with Jon Pearce?" Sarah heard her own tone of voice and realized she was being too sharp with Gary. But since he'd seen how interested she really was in Bernard, she took it out on him.

"No way," he protested. "This shirt was the first one I picked out of the drawer this morning. It's just a coincidence that it happened to be my Makers T-shirt. Anyway, it'll be my outstanding talent that'll convince Jon Pearce that I should be in the music school."

"Yeah, sure," she laughed skeptically.

By this time, at least thirty seniors had already taken seats, waiting for the meeting to begin. As Sarah gazed around the room, she was distressed to see that there were at least five pianists that she knew of, including Naomi Goldman, a super classical pianist who still took lessons from some big teacher in Manhattan, and Paul Dunbar, a very good player who made money on weekends with his own jazz band. She knew they both played better than she did, and if Jon Pearce limited the number of pianists in the music school, there was a fair chance that she wouldn't make it. But she wasn't about to give up yet. If they take at least three pianists, she told herself, I still have a better-than-average chance.

As Sarah was sizing up the competition, Ms. Stillman finally showed up with Jon Pearce. Jon did not exactly look like a rock star, standing by the black board in front of the class. He looked . . . well, normal, Sarah thought as she tried to keep from staring at him. He was very tall, at least 6'3", with longish blond hair falling casually over his collar. His eyes were tiny and very bright, and his smile was infectious. Talking softly with Ms. Stillman, he leaned against the blackboard ledge, his legs crossed and his rust-brown cowboy boots peeking out from under his jeans. He kept his hands thrust deep into the pockets of his khaki-colored sport coat.

A hush came over the room as it soon became evident that everyone was staring at Jon Pearce. Finally, Ms. Stillman turned around and gazed at the class, an expression of mock amazement on her face.

"If I could only get this kind of rapt attention in my History classes. . . . Now that everyone's here, I'll get started. Since I've already explained the objectives of the Junior Professionals' Program in my classes this week, I won't go over it again unless someone has a question. . . . Okay, then. Let me introduce you to our volunteer professional, who will discuss the goals of our music school—Mr. Jon Pearce." She stepped aside and leaned against the windowsill, giving the floor to Maplewood High's favorite son.

Jon Pearce stepped forward slowly and sat on the teacher's desk, dangling his pointy, hand-tooled boots below him. He smiled broadly, which made his eyes crinkle and shine.

"Hi. I'm Jon Pearce." His voice was deep but mellow. "I think some of you are familiar with my work. . . ." He grinned broadly again as several people chuckled at his modesty. "As Ms. Stillman may have already explained to you, the Junior Professionals' Music School is going to have two distinct parts—the teaching of music and the management of the business. Ms. Stillman will supervise the business end, while I take care of the teaching. Ms. Stillman and I plan to work together so that all the student teachers in the music school will be able to understand and operate the total business. You see, although these two aspects of the music school may sometimes seem as different as—well, accounting and music—you'll see that it's really more like one hand washing the other. The teaching of music to kids in the community will be the essential service, but poor business management will make it impossible for us to run the school for more than a couple of weeks.

"I realize that we may seem to be harping on the importance of the business end. Well, we are. Because we want to show you that sound management is the key to success in any business, no matter how much talent you have. Let me give you an example. In 1975, the Makers were unknowns, playing almost exclusively in local clubs in New Jersey. We were very, very good back then, and we also had the talent to record and tour by that time. However, it wasn't until 1978, three years later, that we got a recording contract and really started to succeed. Why did it take us three years to get a single on the charts? Because we had terrible management. Our first manager did not know how to book a rock group. Consequently, we did not play at the right clubs and we weren't being seen by people in the music business. We also lacked a system of money management, so when we did make money, we squandered it. Although it seemed fair simply to split the profits five ways, we never seemed to have any money for new equipment and repairs. In our first three years as a group, we never invested in ourselves, you see. This became painfully evident when we had to cancel a winter gig in Boston because we couldn't afford to replace the bald tires on our van. *This* was when we decided to get our act together. The first thing we did was to hire a good experienced manager. He put us each on a fixed salary and then put aside money for the group. When it came to profits, he treated us like a company, not five individuals. Soon we had built up enough capital to get new equipment, which allowed us to take jobs at bigger and better clubs where we were finally 'discovered' one night by someone from OCI Records.

"The rest is history, but the point I want to impress upon you is that in any kind of venture, you're nothing until you can manage your money properly. It took the Makers some long hard years of struggling to learn that. But if we do it right with our music school, you'll learn it in a couple of months."

He looked around the room, his mouth set grimly for a moment. The class was silent, surprised by this unexpected lecture. Gary seemed shocked to hear his idol talking about business like his father. Sarah was intrigued by his words, eager to hear more about the inner workings of a rock group.

Jon's infectious smile spread across his face again. "Now that I've gotten that out of the way, I'll jump off my soapbox and get to the fun stuff."

Gary's face finally relaxed, and he breathed a sigh of relief. It was music that he wanted to hear about.

"What I plan to do before I hold any auditions for teachers is a little preliminary market research. Because of budget cuts, school music programs have been all but eliminated in the Maplewood system. Jefferson Junior High has no music facilities whatsoever. I happen to know that the going rate for private music lessons is about ten dollars an hour. We're going to charge three dollars a lesson so that the kids who are interested in music, but whose parents can't afford private lessons, will be able to afford our prices.

"But first I want to find out what we've got—how many guitarists, pianists, drummers, bassoonists, whatever. Then I'm going to canvass Jefferson Junior High myself for prospective students to find out just how many students want to take lessons and what instruments they want to learn. You see, it would be ridiculous to have, say, ten guitar teachers and only three or four kids who wanted to learn guitar."

Heads nodded in agreement. No one could argue with his logic. The guitarists in the room just hoped that Jon's example wouldn't hold true.

"This is simply a matter of fitting our supply to the demand. Therefore, I'm going to pass out this questionnaire. Please fill it out now. I want your name, address and phone number. What instrument or instruments you play. If you can read music. And I want to know what days you will be available to teach, including Saturdays." Jon passed out the questionnaires, then went over to the window to stand with Ms. Stillman. The class couldn't hear what she was saying, but she seemed to be complimenting him on his presentation.

"Geez, he sounded like Chrome-Dome for a while there," Gary whispered. "This isn't exactly what I expected."

"Ssshh, tell me later." Sarah was so excited with

the prospects of the music school, she busily began writing as soon as she got her questionnaire. When she got to the question about availability, she put down that she could teach every weekday afternoon and Saturdays. With Steve away at college, she had a lot of time on her hands.

She completed her questionnaire right away. As she waited, she glanced out the window, then gradually turned and looked at Bernard who was gazing out the window himself, apparently having finished his questionnaire, too. Sarah wondered what instrument he played. Either trumpet or cello, she guessed.

"Okay," Jon stepped forward again, "unless anyone needs more time, please pass the forms up to the front."

The sound of shuffling papers was heard through the room. The girl behind Gary tried to hand him a pile, but he was still too busy filling in his questionnaire. It looked as though he were writing an essay. The pile of forms was passed over to Sarah instead, who decided to hold them for a moment until Gary finished writing what she suspected was a fan letter to Jon Pearce. When she glanced down at the pile, she saw that the new boy's questionnaire was on top. She felt self-conscious about reading it, but she couldn't help herself.

His name was Bernard St. Onge, and he lived on Euclid Avenue. He had written down that he played "classical guitar" and that he was available to teach every day, including Saturdays.

A guitarist, she thought, *everyone plays guitar. He*

might not make it into the school. Gary startled her as he suddenly tossed his questionnaire on top of Bernard's. Could he tell that she was reading Bernard's questionnaire? She rapidly evened the stack of papers and handed them to Jon Pearce.

"Thank you," he said softly, and she smiled back bashfully.

"Okay," Jon spoke to the class, "I'm going to start holding auditions next Thursday. Ms. Stillman will let you know where and what time. In the meantime, I'm going to figure out how many teachers we'll need, so regretfully some of you may not even get to audition if I can't find a student who wants to learn the instrument you play. A list of the people I will want to see will be posted by next Tuesday at the latest. As for the audition, please prepare any two pieces of your choice, *but* I do want to hear you play two different types of music—be it classical, rock, jazz, gospel, folk, whatever. Okay? Any questions?"

Paul Dunbar raised his hand.

"Yes?"

"Mr. Pearce, can we use a Makers' song for the audition?"

"Hmmm. . . . Yeah, I guess so. But remember, I may tend to be *more* critical of one of my own pieces than I would of someone else's," he chuckled, obviously pleased to hear that his music was being performed. "If there are no more questions, we can adjourn this meeting and you can go home and practice. Okay?"

He turned toward Ms. Stillman, but several enthusiastic students cut him off, most just wanting to get up close to the famous ex-Maker. Of course, Gary was at the head of the pack.

Sarah, however, remained in her seat, still pondering Bernard St. Onge's questionnaire. *New in school and available for extracurricular activities Monday through Friday, and Saturday, too,* she thought. *Doesn't have a girl friend, I bet.*

When Sarah stood up to leave, she noticed that Jon was surrounded by a group of seven or eight prospective student-teachers. Ms. Stillman was standing by the blackboard, talking to Bernard again. Sarah pictured him bent over his classical guitar, playing a very difficult Bach fugue.

5

Sarah scowled at the gooey mountain of macaroni and cheese before her. If it looks this bad, what does it taste like? she wondered.

"Ummm, that looks fantastic," Penny said sarcastically, as she unwrapped the date-nut bread and cream cheese sandwich she had brought from home. She giggled.

"If you were a pal"—Sarah poked her friend in the ribs—"you would share it with me for half of your sandwich."

"No way. I'll give you half of mine, but please keep yours."

"Thanks, you're a true friend. Say, how was that concert you went to?"

"Oh, don't ask. I don't know why I let Gary drag me to these freak shows."

"Who was it you saw again?"

"Repro. And I was bored stiff. I mean, I just couldn't get into it at all. Gary loved it, of course."

"They are weird. I've seen them on TV a couple of times. Sort of like hypnotized space-shots, aren't they?"

"That's putting it mildly. Besides the fact that they sound like computers to me, they wear these strange pillbox hats that look like red plastic lampshades from the starship *Enterprise*. They were actually selling these stupid hats at the concert. And guess who bought one?"

"Gary?" It was no surprise.

"Oh, he looked so retarded. I could have died sitting with him on the train home."

"Hey, this is pretty good," Sarah said as she took another bite of Penny's sandwich. "Did you make the date-nut bread?"

"Me? The Betty Crocker of Maplewood High? Are you kidding? My mother made it. Don't you remember? I'm the one who can burn water."

"Oh, yeah. I'm still trying forget about those brownies you made during the summer. As a matter of fact, they had about the same consistency as this macaroni and cheese."

Penny frowned down at the spreading yellow mass on Sarah's plate. "Well, that must be because both recipes came from the Official Repro Cookbook."

Sarah laughed as she was swallowing, and for a moment she started to choke. Recovering quickly with a sip of iced tea, she gasped, "Don't make me laugh when I'm trying to eat this stuff!"

"Okay, okay. But there was one good thing about the concert."

"What's that?"

"Because I agreed to go to his stupid concert, Gary broke down and took me to that French movie I like so much. It was at the Ormont on Sunday."

"*The 400 Blows?* You've seen that about fifty times already!"

"Just about. But it's so great. I love that movie," she sighed nostalgically. "Oh, yeah," she just remembered, "guess who was there?"

"Who?"

"Bernard St. Onge, the new guy in school. You know, he's Belgian, not French like we thought."

"Yeah, I know. Gary told me as a matter of fact."

"Really? He didn't tell me! What a jerk!"

"Gary's just not into gossip the way we are. He forgets to tell you the important things. So how did you find out about the mysterious Mr. St. Onge?"

"Do you remember Susan Aronson? She graduated last year."

"Yeah, she was on the prom committee with Steve."

"Well, she was at the movie, too. After it was over, I went over to say hi to her. And as we were talking, Bernard happened to pass by and he gave her a little wave. Well, you know me, I just had to ask how she knew him. It turns out that his family moved in across the street from her."

Euclid Avenue, Sarah instantly recalled the address she had seen on Bernard's questionnaire for the music school. She decided not to mention it, though. Penny might get the wrong idea.

"Susan knew all about his family because Bernard's father is her Political Science professor at the university."

"I thought Susan went away to college."

"She was supposed to, but she changed her mind during the summer. She wasn't sure about going all the way to Colorado, I guess, so she applied to the university here at the last minute. Now she lives at home and commutes to college. Sounds like high school all over again to me."

"I'm sure she had her reasons." Sarah was eager to get back to the subject of Bernard. "So you said one of her teachers is Bernard's father," she prodded.

"Oh, yeah. Well, she found out that they're from Belgium because the prof talks about his 'homeland' a lot in class. She said he's very distinguished, looks a little like Yves Montand."

"Oh, brother. . . ."

"That's what Susan said! He's good-looking, craggy, she said."

"Okay, okay, what else?" Sarah's curiosity was beginning to show.

"Well, Susan said that Bernard's mother seems to be very attractive, except she hasn't really seen her up close. Susan doesn't think they have any other kids besides Bernard. And she mentioned that they have a Peugeot, a French car. Professor St. Onge gave her a lift to school one day. That's when she met Bernard. His father was dropping him off at school that day, too."

"Uh-huh . . . what else?"

"That's it."

"That's it?"

"What do you expect? Do you think Susan sits by her window with binoculars to see what her neighbors are doing? Maybe she goes through their garbage to see what they eat?" Penny giggled.

"Oh. . . ." Sarah seemed disappointed.

"Anyway, how come you're so interested?" Penny fought back a big grin. "You're not . . . ah, you haven't got a crush on Bernard, have you?"

"No, I do not have a crush on anyone," Sarah snapped back.

"Okay, okay! It was just a question. I didn't mean to accuse you or anything."

"Good. Let's drop this business about Bernard. It's just gossip and it makes us sound like old ladies."

"But you're the one who said we—never mind!" Penny figured it wasn't worth arguing about. "I guess you didn't have a very good weekend, huh?"

"No, it was fine. Quiet. Nice."

"Oh . . . good." Penny fingered a strand of her frizzy red hair. She could tell she was treading on thin ice from Sarah's sudden defensiveness.

"I practiced the piano a lot," Sarah offered. "For the music school auditions."

"Oh, yeah. Mrs. Ryan has been complaining that Gary's been playing his drums more than usual. Do you think you'll get into the music school?"

55

"I really don't know. I mean, my playing is fine, but there's some pretty stiff competition. Namely, Paul Dunbar and Naomi Goldman. If they take three or more pianists, I think I've got a good chance. But I know Paul and Naomi will get picked before me."

"Paul I can see. But Naomi Goldman? I mean, I hear she plays great classical music, but come on! She'll scare her pupils to death. She's so serious."

"She's a good pianist, though," Sarah said, "and Mr. Pearce won't exactly be looking for laughs—"

"That's for sure," Penny agreed, "but let's not get uptight about it now. We've got enough to think about. Beside, I've got Chrome-Dome next period."

"Hey, speaking of Chrome-Dome, how's the Junior Professionals' Theater coming along?"

"Not bad actually. I hate to say it, but he's not such a bad guy after all. He's really pretty funny outside of class, and he has great plans for this theater."

"Yeah, tell me."

"Well, we're gonna use the cafeteria for everything, which didn't exactly thrill me, but it's the only space we could get for now. But so what? Every Friday we're going to have a disco, Saturdays will be concerts, and Sunday afternoons will be movies. But we're gonna put on good shows, not the usual amateur-night stuff."

"So you're getting Miss Edwards to read selections from the best term papers she's ever graded?"

"No kidding, Sarah. The discos will each have a different theme. The first one will be Rap Night, a week from this Friday. Mr. Ciofi—that's our volunteer advisor—he's getting us good contacts with booking agents so that we can get decent groups for the concert. Our plan is to make enough money from the discos, the movies, and the concerts so that we can hire a hall and get some big-name act to play."

"Who do you have in mind?"

"Well, obviously we won't be able to afford Bruce Springsteen, Billy Joel, the Makers, or anyone like that. But we'd like to get someone who'll attract a big crowd."

"How about Repro?" Sarah chided.

"Forget it! Seeing them once is enough for me. But you know what I mean. We'll have to get a group who's had a hit, but hasn't played the Garden for twelve dollars a seat yet."

"I see—so is your job to find this big act for your big concert?"

"No, that's a long way off and still in the planning stage. I'm on the movie committee. We're going to pick films that will be shown on Sunday afternoons. Mr. Ciofi has gotten us in touch with a couple of film distribution companies and we're waiting to get their catalogues now. Gee, I hope we can get *The 400 Blows*."

"Hey, you could put together the perfect double feature for you and Gary—*The 400 Blows* and *Enter the Dragon* with Bruce Lee." Sarah mimed a karate chop into her pile of macaroni and cheese.

"Very funny." Penny made a face at Sarah's suggestion, then she looked up and her eyes widened a bit. "Hey, look who's coming this way."

Sarah turned toward the lunch line where Penny

indicated, and there was Lisa Forster at the cashier. As usual, she looked as though she were off to the country club—oxblood penny loafers, beige baggies, a button-down, blue broadcloth shirt, and a navy blazer. As Sarah scrutinized her preppy ensemble, she suddenly realized that it was practically the same outfit Bernard had worn on the first day of school. Jealously, Sarah wondered whether it was just a coincidence.

"Will you look at what's on her tray!" Penny whispered behind her hand.

Sarah stifled a derisive laugh when she spotted the steaming pile of orange-yellow macaroni and cheese even larger than her own.

"She kills me, she really does," Penny murmured. "Get a load of the barrettes. She's got them pulled so tight, she looks Oriental." Unconsciously, Penny twisted a long strand of her own frizzy hair around her finger.

"She's coming this way. You don't think she's going to lower herself to eat with the commoners? I mean we're not dressed right, are we?" Sarah put on a British accent and tilted her head haughtily.

"I'm afraid you're right, my dear," Penny whispered as Lisa walked down the aisle, trying to catch Penny's eye.

"Do you mind if I sit here?" Lisa flashed a condescending smile. When Lisa set down her plate of macaroni and cheese, Penny made a face and rolled her eyes, and Sarah almost burst out laughing. "Sarah, Penny, how are your classes going?"

"Fine," Penny said, unwilling to elaborate.

"Okay. Some good, some not so good," Sarah offered.

"Say, are you two participating in the Junior Professionals' thing? I think it's just marvelous!"

"Yes, as a matter of fact. Penny's working with the theater, and I'm auditioning for the music school."

"Oh. . . ." Lisa made it obvious that she was unimpressed. She dug into her macaroni and cheese with unusual gusto, especially for someone who always claimed to be on a diet. Watching her eat, Penny continued to mug with bulging eyes. Sarah had to bite the insides of her cheeks to keep from laughing out loud. "Well," Lisa said after swallowing hard, "I'm on the Junior Professionals' Stock Brokerage Firm."

"Really? I don't think I've heard about that one," Penny chirped in a haughty singsong.

"Oh, it's very exciting, Penny. We're going to learn how to make sound investments, follow the trends, play the market. You know."

"Sounds boring to me."

"Not at all, Penny. Of course, they're not going to let us use real money initially. We'll negotiate with Monopoly money at first, so that we can perfect our investment skills, following the stocks we pretend to buy and calculate our profits . . . or losses if there are any. I really wanted to use real money. I mean that would really be a rush, don't you think? I told our advisor that my father would gladly give me $500 to invest, but he said absolutely not. He said I didn't know enough yet to invest it wisely. That it wouldn't be fair to the other kids because they couldn't all come up with $500 to invest too. Can you imagine? I mean, your father's an officer at a bank, Sarah—wouldn't he give you at least five hundred for this kind of thing?"

"Ah . . . I. . . ." Sarah felt pressured by Lisa's question. Her family certainly wasn't poor, but she knew they probably couldn't afford to just give her that much money to play with. Lisa loved to flaunt her wealth, especially around kids whose parents weren't nearly as well off as the Forsters, who owned several companies and a resort in the Caribbean. It was stupid to compete like this, and the longer Sarah hesitated in answering Lisa, the more upset she became with herself. "No, I don't think he would give me that much money, Lisa. Not when I didn't know how to invest it properly."

"Oh. . . ." Lisa's nose was in the air as she tossed another forkful of macaroni and cheese into her mouth. Sarah could feel the frost forming on Lisa's manner now that she felt she had established her superiority.

"Five hundred dollars," Penny said in amazement, shaking her head. "I could just imagine what my father'd do if I asked him for that much money! He'd think I'd gone nuts!"

"He just might be right," Sarah observed with a grin.

Lisa pursed her lips disapprovingly, then suddenly changed the subject. "Say, Sarah, what do you hear from Steve? Does he just love Cornell?"

"Ah . . . yeah, I guess he likes it. Haven't . . . heard much from him."

"Oh, really?" Lisa moaned with phony concern, "You don't think he's going out with a college girl, do you?"

Sarah's cheeks flushed with anger. She couldn't be certain whether it was Lisa's catty remark or the possible truth her question contained that made her more furious. Naturally, it had crossed her mind more than a few times that Steve might find another girlfriend at Cornell. But Sarah had never spoken it out loud, she had never actually heard the awful possibility expressed in words. Hearing it now from Lisa Forster of all people made her see red.

"I doubt it, Lisa." She forced herself to remain composed. "Steve's not that way. I know him."

"Well, of course. Steve is a doll. Everybody knows that. But, you know, living away from home for the first time and all, guys do tend to get wild. My brother tells me that there are no curfews or parietals at his dorm at Yale." There was a cruel glint in Lisa's eye.

"What are parietals?" Penny asked.

"It's the dorm rule that limits the times when girls can be in boys' dorms and boys in girls' dorms. There aren't too many schools that have them anymore. Do you know if Cornell still has parietals, Sarah? Or are all the dorms co-ed?"

"I don't know," Sarah said firmly, still struggling to contain herself.

"Well, I'm sure they don't, but so what. You said Steve's not that kind of guy." Lisa stood up suddenly and picked up her tray. "Sorry, I've got to run. This macaroni and cheese was really pretty poor," she commented, tilting her plate which now had no more than a couple of forkfuls left from the original yellow mountain. "Bye-ee!"

Penny made a face at Lisa's departing back. Sarah was on the verge of tears.

6

That Saturday Penny borrowed her mother's car so that she and Sarah could go to the mall. Neither of the girls really needed to buy anything, but Penny felt that Sarah could use a little cheering up, and shopping might do the trick.

It was obvious to Penny that Sarah was not adjusting very well to being without Steve. This week had been particularly rough on her, what with no word from Steve yet, Lisa Forster's cutting remarks, and Sarah's nightly practice marathons on the piano for her upcoming audition. Sarah was a silent sufferer, never mentioning how bad all this was really making her feel. But Penny knew her well enough to see that she needed a break.

When Penny called her on Saturday morning to see if she would like to go to the mall, Sarah immediately protested. "Ah, no . . . I don't think so, Penny. I have to practice for the audition."

"You can practice later," Penny persisted.

"I'm too rusty, I have to spend all—"

"You can spare a couple of hours. I'll pick you up after lunch."

"But—"

"No buts. I'll be at your house at one."

But when Penny picked her up, she was shocked to see how haggard Sarah looked. It was a pretty good guess that she was trying to forget her problems by losing herself in her music. But it was obvious that she was overdoing it. Still Penny decided that it would be best if she treated Sarah as if nothing were wrong. Sarah just had to snap out of this depression by herself, that was the important thing.

"Where shall we go first?" Penny asked as she pulled her mother's Volkswagen into a parking space and turned off the ignition.

"I don't care. You pick." Sarah was smiling, but her voice was listless.

"Okay, you asked for it. And don't say I didn't give you a chance." Penny got out of the car and locked the door behind her.

"What are you talking about? Where do *you* want to go?" Sarah shaded her eyes from the glaring sun as she stared at Penny across the roof of the Volkswagen.

"How could you forget? My favorite store!"

In unison, they both exclaimed, "The Designers' Den!" and with that Sarah seemed to perk up a bit.

When they got inside, Penny began running up and down the aisles searching through the racks at random. It wasn't exactly clear to Sarah what Penny was shopping for because first she tried on a vested suit, then a few tops, then a pair of very tight designer cords. But Sarah was really taken aback when Penny emerged from the dressing room in a skimpy, black satiny disco dress with a slit that went to the top of her thigh. She was still wearing her beat-up running shoes with this sexy dress, and the effect was something like watching the "Beverly Hillbillies."

"What do you think?" Penny giggled, striking a pose with one hand on her hip, the other behind her head.

"It's . . . ah . . . really something." Sarah was biting the insides of her cheeks again.

"Well, as Rod Stewart says, 'Do you think I'm sexy?' "

"Well. . . ." Sarah screwed up her face, trying to figure out how to be truthful and diplomatic at the same time.

"Come on, come on. Say it!"

"Let's just say that it's not you."

"Really? Why? What's wrong with it?"

Confronted with so much bare skin—back, arms, chest and legs—Sarah couldn't contain herself. "Well—now don't take this the wrong way—but you look like . . . a freckle farm." Immediately Sarah slapped a hand over her mouth to stifle a laugh.

"*A freckle farm?*" Penny looked at her arms and shoulders as if someone had just splattered paint over them, then she let out a shriek of uncontrollable laughter. "You're really a stitch, Sarah. You know that? I've got to take this thing off before I split it."

While Penny was in the dressing room, changing back into her jeans, Sarah started looking through a rack of sport jackets. A fire-engine red wool blazer with gold embossed buttons caught her eye. She picked up the sleeve and saw that it was her size. Why not? she thought, taking it off the rack to try it on. When Penny returned from the dressing room, Sarah was standing before the three-way mirror, examining her image in the red blazer.

"You're not going to buy *that,* are you?" Penny groaned, coming up from behind.

"Why? What's wrong with it?"

"It's too preppy. You look like you're going to a fox hunt."

"You say *preppy* as if it were a dirty word. I think some of those styles are okay."

"So do I. As a matter of fact, I love button-down, broadcloth shirts, especially white ones. But there's a certain preppy attitude I can't take."

"You mean as in Lisa Forster?"

"Exactly. The way she puts on airs about her country club and her friends at Yale and playing the stock market, even the stupid way she talks with all her teeth showing—yuk! I mean, everybody knows she's rich, she doesn't have to advertise."

"I agree. She and her buddies use their preppy clothes like brand-name labels, making sure everybody is super-aware that they're high class."

"Yeah, well, I'm not very impressed. You ought to hear some of the dumb things Lisa says in class. I swear Mr. Shapiro is so fed up he ignores her when she raises her hand in math because he knows her questions are always so stupid. As far as I'm concerned, she's just another dumb blonde."

"And not even a natural dumb blonde!" Sarah took off the jacket and suddenly noticed the designer label sewn over the inside pocket. Stamped across the fancy green and gold label was the word SECOND in big black letters.

"Ha!" Penny grinned sarcastically. "Just like ole Lisa—a high-class second."

"Come on, let's get out of here before we get as catty as she is." Sarah went to hang up the jacket.

"Okay. Where now?"

"Let's go to Melody Mart," Sarah suggested. "I want to get something."

"Hey, look! There's a new Blondie album out." Penny rushed to the display bin where dozens of Blondie albums were lined up in tiers.

"Hmmm. . . ." Sarah picked one up and scrutinized the list of songs on the back cover.

"Gary's already heard this. He says it's pretty good."

"No . . . I don't think so. I've only got enough money for one album and there's something else I want to get."

Sarah peered down the long aisles that were filled with hundreds and hundreds of albums—mostly rock, arranged alphabetically from ABBA to ZZ

Top. She walked briskly down the rock aisle, gazing at all the wild cover art as she passed. At the end of the aisle, she made a sour face. Then she spotted a sign against the far wall that said CLASSICAL with an arrow pointing straight down. *That's it,* she thought.

Tagging behind like a faithful puppy, Penny followed a taciturn Sarah, surprised to see her heading away from the rock section. Gradually she made her way up behind Sarah who was staring at the dividers in the bins and looking confused.

"What're you looking for?" Penny suddenly asked.

"Oh!"—Sarah was startled—"ah . . . a record."

"Really? I thought we were here for bagels," she grimaced. "Maybe it's me."

"I'm looking for a classical record. Okay?"

"Fine with me. It's just that I can't remember you ever buying anything but rock. I thought your mother already had every opera and symphony ever recorded."

"I'm not looking for an opera or a symphony." Sarah's voice sounded a bit testy. "I'm, ah . . . looking for something that I may want to use for my audition. See, I have to get the record to . . . make sure that I'm playing it right."

"Oh." Penny just stood there.

Trying to ignore her, Sarah turned and started sifting through the closest bin, which happened to be the Wagner section. She hoped Penny would go away for a while, but her friend just stood there as if she were waiting for a bus. Why doesn't she go back to the rock section? Sarah said to herself. Then she flipped over yet another album and came to one with a plain white cover and tiny nondescript printing all in German. She pulled it out of the bin.

"Ever hear this?" she asked Penny matter-of-factly.

"Huh? Are you kidding?" Penny made a face. "The closest I come to classical music is Chuck Berry."

"Oh . . . well then, I don't know whether I should get this or—"

"Sarah, I'll be in the rock section. Come get me when you're ready."

"Okay, Sarah sighed, secretly relieved to see Penny go.

Alone at last, Sarah started looking through the records of several composers—Bach, Beethoven, Mozart, Mahler—but she couldn't find what she wanted. Frantically, she started flipping through the bins at random, investigating composers she had never even heard of.

"Can I help you?" A voice came from over her shoulder.

"Huh?" she gasped as if she had been caught doing something wrong.

"Is there anything in particular you're looking for?" It was a store clerk, a man in his early thirties, almost entirely bald but with a great bushy red beard that couldn't cover his smile. "Maybe I can help you find what you want."

"Oh, yes. I'm looking for a good classical guitar record."

"Okay, you're looking in the wrong place. Go up to that section"—he pointed farther up the aisle—"on the left and you'll see albums arranged by instrument instead of composer. There's a whole section devoted to guitar."

"Thank you." She rushed to the bins he indicated and started flipping through the albums, hoping that the right jacket would jump out at her. Unfortunately, she knew very little about classical guitarists and guitar composers, and the jackets weren't very much help to her. Flustered, she looked back at the clerk and timidly waved him over.

"Can't find what you want?" he asked as he walked up to her.

"The problem is I'm not sure what I want."

"Oh. . . ." He scratched his beard, trying to understand.

"See, I have this . . . friend who plays classical guitar and I'd like to get a record that covers a few different periods of guitar music. You know, something that I can study so I won't be a complete dummy if we ever talk about classical guitar. Does that make sense to you?" Sarah was slightly embarrassed as the clerk just continued to stroke his beard.

"Yeah"—he bobbed his head up and down—"that makes sense." He turned to the bin and started searching through the guitar section until he found what he was looking for. "Segovia!" he declared. "The grand master of the guitar. Your friend will be impressed with this if he's a serious classical guitarist."

"Oh, yes, he's very serious." Sarah was taken

aback for a moment. It seemed strange but tantalizing to be referring to Bernard so intimately.

"Then I suggest you take this Segovia record. It has music by several different composers—all fine guitar pieces. And the performance is—well, Segovia is always superb."

Sarah took the album from the clerk and checked out the selections. DeVisée, Sor, Carcassi, Guiliani, Carulli. She was unfamiliar with most of the composers, but the clerk's recommendation was enough to convince her that this was a good choice. Pursing her lips and nodding as she looked it over, she finally thanked the clerk and walked briskly to the cashier. She quickly paid for the record while Penny was preoccupied in the rock section and breathed a sigh of relief when the album was finally sealed in the bag. Then she went to get Penny.

"What do you say? Ready to go?"

"Yup. Hey! What did you get?"

"Oh . . . I finally found what I wanted."

"So what is it?"

"Segovia."

Penny shrugged. Classical music was all a mystery to her. "Come on. Let's get something to eat. I'm starved."

"A slice of pizza and a Coke, please," Sarah ordered at the stand-up pizza counter on the mall's upper level near Sears.

"Yeah, same for me, please," Penny interjected.

A few minutes later the gray-haired woman behind the counter brought them their order.

"Let's take that bench." Penny pointed to an empty spot by the glass railing. "We can eat and watch the people downstairs."

"You mean you want to check out the guys?"

"Whatever." Penny grinned. "Come on."

Balancing their cups and paper plates while clutching their pocketbooks and packages under their arms, they walked carefully over to the bench and get themselves settled. Sarah placed her record by her side at the end of the bench away from Penny and put her leather bag on top of it.

"This is pretty good," Penny commented after her first bite of pizza.

Sarah took a bit and considered it as she chewed, her brows knit. "Not bad, not bad at all. But not as good as Guido's in Maplewood Village."

"Well, what'd you expect? Nobody makes pizza like Guido." Penny gestured with her closed hand the same way Guido himself did whenever he pulled a fresh creation from his oven.

Sarah chuckled, then they both became quiet as they worked on their pizza. A welcome change, Sarah felt, for Penny was rarely quiet.

"Will you look at that!" Penny suddenly blurted, her mouth still full.

"What?"

"Down there! At the Levi's store! I don't believe this. I think I'm gonna die right here!"

"What are you talking about?"

Sarah didn't want to believe her eyes, but she had to. It was painfully true. From where she sat, Sarah had a bird's-eye view of Lisa Forster standing at a table full of jeans, sorting through them with Bernard.

Sarah's cheeks began to burn. She felt confused. She couldn't figure out if she was more upset with Lisa for being so awful, Bernard for falling into the preppy queen's clutches, or herself for feeling the way she did. After all, what right did she have being jealous—she hadn't even met Bernard yet! But then she wanted to kick herself for not being more aggressive. I could have introduced myself at the music school meeting, she regretted. But there was no use going over what she could have done. It was clear that Lisa was getting tight with him. When a guy lets you help him buy clothes, he must like you—everyone knows that. Sarah didn't want to look at the two of them anymore, but she couldn't help herself. As she glared down at Lisa, she began to imagine the details of their day together—Lisa showing Bernard around the mall, pretending to be just friendly when she really had something else in mind. Then they'd probably drive to Don's for lunch, and then . . . Sarah didn't want to think about it.

"She's incredible!" Penny whispered. "School's open just one week and she's already out on patrol. Figures that she'd go after him. The continental type. What a . . ."

Sarah wished Penny would shut up for once. But she couldn't even tell her to be quiet, her throat was so constricted. Abruptly, she got up and dumped the rest of her pizza and Coke into a nearby trash can. Penny got up and disposed of her trash, too.

"Well, shall we go? I don't particularly want to

run into her and have her flaunt her latest conquest like one of her gifts from 'Daddy.'"

"Yeah, let's go," Sarah mumbled.

But as she bent down to pick up her things, she was suddenly angry with herself for having wasted six dollars on a classical guitar album. She felt like leaving it there. Or flinging it over the railing. But not wanting to reveal her true feelings to Penny, she picked up the humiliating package and silently left the mall with Penny still jabbering away.

At least, I still have Steve, she thought. *I hope.*

7

Sarah?" Mrs. Jordan stood at the bottom of the stairway, one hand on the banister. "Dinner's ready, Sarah. Come on down."

"Be right there," the muffled reply emerged from the dim hallway.

Sarah got up from her reading chair and switched off the lamp in her room. She placed her book—*The Rainbow* by D. H. Lawrence—face down on her seat. As she bent over, she caught a glimpse of the unopened Melody Mart bag leaning against the wall. Sarah turned away quickly and left the room, resolved to return the Segovia record as soon as possible.

By the time Sarah arrived, her parents and her brother David were already seated in the dining room. Mrs. Jordan was beaming with pride and satisfaction. With David now in his sophomore year at Columbia, these family dinners were becoming a rare event since David couldn't always make the time to come home. Sarah was beginning to miss him too, even though they had often squabbled like cats and dogs when they were living under the same roof. Now she wished he were back again. Between Steve and Bernard, she had a lot of questions about male behavior, and there was no better counselor than her older brother, she felt. David had the kind of open face that made people want to confide in him. Sarah always found his warm brown eyes and trusting smile reassuring. She'd been trying to talk to him alone ever since he'd come in on Friday night. But between her mother's efforts to ply him with "good, home-cooked meals" and her father's endless questions about college, poor Sarah couldn't get a word in edgewise. She realized she could call him at his dorm when he got back, but it just wasn't the kind of thing you could discuss over the phone. Anyway it was a long distance call and she'd have to explain to her parents why she rang up such a big bill to speak to David. The situation was too embarrassing even to risk lying about. Unfortunately, David was the only person she could trust, the only one who could help her because he was both understanding and a member of the opposite sex. But if she didn't corner him after dinner tonight, she'd be out of luck. There was no way of knowing when he'd be back, and he had to leave tonight because he had an early class on Mondays.

"Sarah, would you like to carve?" Mrs. Jordan asked, indicating the roast.

"Sure, Mom." Sarah went to the sideboard and began her attack on the big roast beef, pleased with the extra-sharp carving knife and the picture-perfect slices she could cut with it. As she worked on the roast, her father continued his interrogation of her brother.

"So how do you feel about changing your major to pre-law, David?" Mr. Jordan had only one facial expression—serious concern. That look was a classic in the Jordan house—knit brows, anxious eyes, set mouth, and a tiny bit of sweat glistening just behind his receding hairline. Tom Jordan's face was a constant. Whether he was considering a customer's loan request at the bank, questioning his son about school, asking his wife what was for dinner, or complimenting his daughter on her piano playing, his expression was always the same.

"Okay. Pre-law is okay." David's answers to his father's intense questions were usually inscrutable. Not because David wasn't talkative or friendly, but because he liked to tease his father and he knew that his mother and sister got a kick out of seeing Mr. Jordan flustered by his vague responses.

"Oh . . . just okay? Nothing else? Anything in particular you like or dislike? Any inclination as to what kind of law you'd like to practice? Criminal, corporate, and so on. Hmmm?" Mr. Jordan's earnestness was not easily deflected.

David pursed his lips, ran his hand through his straight, dark hair, and looked up at the ceiling for a moment, considering the question. Finally he answered. "Nope."

"Well . . . I see. Do you have any ideas about where you'd like to apply to law school then? Do you think you'll—"

"Dad," David interrupted gently, "I've only been in pre-law for a month. Besides, I'm still a sophomore. There'll be plenty of time to consider law schools and law practices. I mean, my classes haven't even begun to scratch the surface. You wouldn't want me to decide about my career without knowing all the options and implications of a law profession. Would you?"

"Ah . . . no. Of course not."

David's sensible attitude was hard to argue with, and succeeded in keeping his father's relentless inquisitiveness at bay, at least temporarily.

"Here you go!" Sarah announced as she laid the serving platter full of perfect slices of juicy roast beef on the table. "Dig in!"

Bowls of rice and broccoli rotated around the table; rolls were distributed; salt, pepper and butter passed. Eventually the only sound in the room was that of silverware against the plates.

"Well, it must be good," Mrs. Jordan finally said, "no one's complaining."

"Excellent, Mom."

"Right . . . it's good. And better than dorm food any day."

"Very good, honey," Mr. Jordan chimed in. "By the way, Sarah, I meant to ask you about your

Junior Professionals' Music School. How's that going?"

"Yes, Sarah, did you tell David about the music school?" Mrs. Jordan jumped in, hoping to temper the fatherly inquisition. "That rock 'n' roll star from town is organizing the program, David. What's his name? I forget."

"Jon Pearce," Mr. Jordan stated flatly before tossing a chunk of broccoli into his mouth.

The other three were stunned to hear this. It was hard to imagine that Mr. Jordan had even heard of rock 'n' roll.

"Gee, Dad, how do you know about the Makers?" David asked.

Mr. Jordan grinned slyly. "One of the bank's best customers. As a matter of fact, just this week we had a nice discussion about a mortgage on a house he's considering." Nonchalantly he speared another piece of roast beef and threw Sarah a smug glance as he lifted it to his mouth.

"Hmmm. . . ." Sarah was suspicious. "I don't suppose you discussed the music school?"

"Nope." It was Mr. Jordan's turn to be inscrutable. "We were talking mortgages. And, of course, I didn't want him to think I'd give his loan application special treatment if he gave you preferential consideration at the music school."

"Thanks, Dad, I appreciate that. But I don't think Jon's that kind of guy. He seems very fair-minded."

"Good. I'm glad to hear it." Father and daughter grinned at each other.

"Hold on!" David broke in. "Will somebody tell me what you're talking about?"

"The Junior Professionals' Music School," Sarah said.

"So what's that?" David asked.

"The Junior Professionals' Program gives seniors at Maplewood High the opportunity to run their own businesses. There are about a dozen different businesses, and the music school is one of them."

"That's the one you're in?"

"Not yet. I still have to pass the audition next week."

"Okay, I'm following you so far. Now what does Jon Pearce have to do with all this?"

"Well, each group has a professional volunteer from the community. Jon Pearce is the volunteer advisor for the music school."

"Wow! It must be great even to have an ex-rock star for an advisor."

"Only temporarily out of the limelight, though," Mr. Jordan commented, and again his children were astonished by his wealth of information about Jon Pearce.

"What do you mean 'only temporarily'?" David asked.

"Well, we did discuss his future plans. After all, the bank does have to know how he intends to pay off his mortgage."

"So are you going to keep us in suspense all night or are you going to tell us?" Sarah was dying to know.

"Oh, no, Sarah. This was a confidential meeting. I can't disclose his plans. It would be unethical."

"Oh, you!" she pouted. "You shouldn't have brought it up if you weren't going to tell us the details."

"Well, you're right about that. Hmmm . . . let's just say that the music industry has not heard the last of Mr. Pearce."

"He's starting a new group?" David guessed.

"'Ask me no questions . . .'" Mr. Jordan began.

"I'll bet he's starting his own record label. A lot of groups do that when they get big," Sarah speculated.

"And he's buying a big house here in Maplewood so that he can set up his own recording studio. Right, Dad? He's putting together his own studio for his label." David was sure he'd solved the mystery.

Mr. Jordan frowned at his two children and let out a heavy sigh. "This is all conjecture on your part. If you share your opinions with anyone"—he looked right at Sarah—"be sure to say that it's your considered *opinion* and not a news leak from your dear father. Understood?"

His stern mood brought an awkward silence to the table. But Sarah changed that at once.

"Don't worry, Dad," she giggled. "We won't tell anybody you're into rock 'n' roll gossip."

"David, what time are you leaving?" Sarah asked as she finished loading the dishwasher.

"About nine-thirty. I'm getting a ride from one of the guys in my dorm who lives in South Orange."

"Oh. . . ." Sarah wanted to ask him about her problems with Steve, but she didn't exactly know how to start.

"What's the matter? You look like you have something on your mind."

"No, no. Not really."

David was always sensitive to other people's feelings. Sarah knew that he suspected there was a problem.

"Tell me, what is college like for freshmen?" she began casually.

"How do you mean?"

"I mean is the workload so tremendous that you don't have time for much else? Or is it like *Animal House*—a lot of drinking beer and partying? You know what I mean?"

"Well, it's a little of both actually. I mean, the school work is a lot harder than high school ever was. But for the kids who are away from home for the first time, living in the dorms, it can get pretty wild. A lot of horsing around and parties and stuff. Some people go overboard, but most straighten out after a while because the work catches up with you eventually. For most kids, either you spend most of your time in the library or you flunk out."

"I see." Sarah wasn't aware that her face was a mask of deep concern, not unlike her father's usual expression.

"Why do you ask? Are you thinking about going away to college next year?"

"Well, yes, I am. But that's not really why I wanted to know."

"Yeah . . . ?" David leaned up against the kitchen counter and folded his arms over his chest. He knew something was up, but he wasn't going to force his sister to talk about it if she wasn't ready.

"Well . . . it's Steve. I haven't heard from him yet and I've been wondering why."

"And you suspect that he might be living it up at Cornell, and forgetting about you in the meantime."

"Something like that," she admitted reluctantly. "I'm afraid he might have found a college girl."

"Hmmm . . . I suppose that's a possibility."

"The rat!" she hissed in her hurt and anger.

"Wait a minute! I didn't say he *did* have another girl friend. I just said it was a possibility. Don't you think you should give Steve the benefit of the doubt? Have you written to him?"

"He promised to write first! I've given him two weeks just to send a postcard! What else can I do?"

"Listen. You may be drawing all the wrong conclusions. When I was a freshman last year, there was another freshman on my floor named Bill who had a girlfriend back home still in high school. They really liked each other a lot, but she started to get suspicious of him when he couldn't write or call as often as she wanted him to.

"See, Bill was a Chemistry major and the work was tremendous. I mean, there were many Friday nights when poor Bill would stumble into the dorm, dead on his feet, while all the other guys were out or just hanging around drinking beer. His girlfriend back home figured he had another girlfriend for sure, and she finally accused him of being unfaithful.

Bill was never able to convince her that it was really the lab work that was taking up all his time. By the end of first semester, they broke up.''

"Yeah, but what about the guy who lived next door to you last year?" Sarah's expression was skeptical.

"Joe? Yes, well, Joe was the other side of the coin. He came from a very strict family and he had gone to an all-male high school. Naturally when he got to college, he went wild. He used to stay up all night, sleep till noon, date a different girl practically every night, drink like a fish—a real party animal. He was really like a dog that had been tied up in the backyard all his life suddenly set free. But it caught up with him. I heard he got straight Ds first semester and he was put on probation. After Christmas break, he was a different guy, though. Quiet and conscientious. Still a party animal, but only on weekends."

"All right, but what about Steve? How do I know he still thinks of us as a couple? How can I find out if he's gone crazy like Joe did?"

"You can't find out. You've just got to be patient. College is a big adjustment to make. You're suddenly responsible for yourself, and that can be pretty scary. Some people treat college like high school without anybody checking up on them, and they end up hurting themselves like Joe did. Other people simply can't handle not having a lot of supervision, so they drop out and go home. You've just got to realize that Steve's probably pretty confused right now with all these changes, and he needs this time to get himself together. I really don't think he'd hurt you on purpose, but people do change, of course. I'd say the only thing you can do is sit tight, maybe write to him, and give him a few more weeks to get in touch with you."

"Maybe you're right," she sighed. "When he's ready to handle college *and* a girlfriend, he'll call me." Sarah did not sound absolutely convinced, but she was willing to consider David's opinion.

But then as she thought of the other possibility— waiting and waiting for Steve, then being rejected— her throat tightened and the tears welled up again.

8

David's advice turned out to be little consolation to Sarah. In fact, his portrayal of life in a college dormitory began to haunt her, keeping her up nights. She imagined scenes of wild, late-night beer blasts attended by dozens of Lisa Forster clones and a devilishly drunken Steve Dowd right in the middle of them all. She knew she was being ridiculous, but she couldn't help it. On Monday after school, she decided to write him a letter and ask him point blank why he hadn't written to her. But then the pen froze in her hand—how could she be accusatory when she didn't know what was really going on with him? What if he really was having a hard time adjusting? If that was the case, he was already having enough problems. He wouldn't need her nagging him now.

She considered writing him a short, chatty note or

sending him a humorous card. She even went to the Hallmark store on Monday night to buy a Snoopy card or something similar. But facing the rows and rows of clever messages and silly cartoons, she just couldn't bring herself to pick one out. Perhaps she was being stupidly proud, but she refused to write to him first. He had promised her just before he left that he'd write to her, and if he loved her, he would keep his promise.

That night she quietly sat down at the piano to practice for her audition. For hours, she played scales and exercises, then a variety of classical pieces. She was still undecided about which classical piece she would use for her audition, but she had narrowed it down to three—one by Mozart, one by Chopin, and one by Beethoven. The Mozart and the Chopin selections were fairly difficult and she could play them pretty well but not magnificently. The Beethoven piece, "Für Elise," was considerably easier, and she knew she played it very well. The problem was that Sarah could not decide whether it would be better to perform brilliantly with an old saw that everyone knew or to risk coming off like a mediocre musician with a more difficult piece. Her first impulse was to do the intense Mozart and try to impress Jon Pearce with her technical mastery of the selection. Then she changed her mind and figured the ghostly melody of the Chopin piece would linger in Jon's mind, giving her a better chance of being chosen.

But then she thought of Naomi Goldman, and her heart sank. Naomi played Chopin better than Chopin! What if Naomi auditioned with the same piece? Sarah wondered in panic. The comparison would be pathetic! Perhaps she should resign herself to "Für Elise," and hope that her mastery of this corny but pretty piece would at least keep her in the competition.

But while Sarah concentrated on her classical selection, she was more casual in her preparation of her other piece—"You've Got a Friend" by Carole King. She had been playing it for years, and people always complimented her whenever she played it. It was a hopeful, upbeat song and she was comfortable with the music, so she wasn't worried about using it for her audition. This song always brought back memories of how close she and Steve used to be and the things they had done together—parties, concerts, plays, the quiet evenings by themselves. Now when she played the song, it was sad and desperate, a plea for friendship rather than an offer.

On Tuesday morning, the music school audition list was posted. Sarah's audition was scheduled for Thursday at 3:15. She was a bit upset to see that Bernard's audition was right after hers, figuring that Lisa Forster would be hanging around just being her obnoxious self. Sarah was nervous enough about the audition, she didn't need Lisa around to aggravate her and Bernard to . . . distract her. Forcing herself to forget about Bernard spending time with Lisa, she scanned the audition list again, looking for the two outstanding pianists in school, Naomi Goldman and Paul Dunbar. Paul's audition was set for Friday at 2:45, and Naomi's was right after his. Good, she thought, maybe they'll cancel each other out or something. Then thinking more realistically, Sarah began to mull over the possibility that this scheduling could affect her own chances. Jon may be overwhelmed hearing those two back to back, and he'll just pick them immediately. Of course, it would work the other way. You have to play two different styles of music. If Paul plays a classical piece, Naomi will make him look bad; if Naomi plays anything popular, Paul is sure to make her look bad. Of course, they have the advantage of auditioning on Friday. They'll be fresher in Jon's mind when he picks the teachers over the weekend . . .

All day long she pondered the situation, trying to psych-out Jon, Paul and Naomi. The crux of the problem seemed to be her classical piece—should she do her shaky Chopin or Mozart and risk the comparison with Naomi, or settle for the Beethoven and try to present herself as a competent, complete musician who could teach any type of music? Finally, when she sat down at the piano to practice that night, she made up her mind. She would perform the Beethoven, hoping that she would impress Jon as someone who understood the nature of music in general and therefore could teach it. Good performers don't always make good teachers, she reassured herself as she started running through her scales to limber up.

The auditions were being held in the music room on the deserted fourth floor of Maplewood High. There were several rooms up there that were seldom used, and it had been decided that the music room would be the logical location for the music school once it got underway. Ever since old Mr. Barker, the music teacher, died a few years ago, the music room just collected dust because the school couldn't afford to hire a replacement. Some of the other teachers made feeble attempts at organizing choirs or marching bands, but the ventures always fell through. Sarah's mother confirmed many people's feelings when she said that Jon Pearce and the Junior Professionals' Music School were a godsend. Not only because they brought musical activities back to the high school, but also because they would offer reasonably priced music lessons to the junior high students whose music teacher had been laid off two years ago.

As Sarah climbed the stairs to the fourth floor, she thought about the program and what a good idea the music school was. Clutching an armful of loose sheet music and music books, she was no longer dreading her audition, and all but a few of the butterflies had flown out of her stomach. After she had stopped worrying about the competition and started concentrating on her two pieces, she had become more confident in her musical ability and more hopeful of her chances of getting picked. She found that practicing for several hours at a stretch was relaxing and satisfying. When she played, the music washed over her like a warm, soothing wave and she was almost able to forget about Steve.

The hallway was empty and silent, only Sarah's

self-conscious footsteps reverberated lightly over the marble floor. It seemed odd that it was so quiet, somebody was supposed to be auditioning now. Is this the right day? she wondered in sudden panic. She approached the music room with trepidation. Slowly she tiptoed up to the door and carefully peered in.

Sitting in a student desk, his head bent over a book, Jon Pearce was lost in his reading. Sarah was surprised to see him there all alone. He was wearing glasses and looked so . . . well, ordinary, just a regular guy, not like the lead guitarist of the Makers. Eventually he noticed her in the doorway. He looked up, peered over his glasses, and smiled warmly. Standing up and extending his hand to her, he suddenly didn't look so ordinary anymore. Her knees got a little weaker as she realized she was shaking hands with a genuine rock star, someone whose face she had seen on thousands of album covers and countless TV shows.

"Hi," he said softly, "you must be Sarah."

"Hi . . . uh, yes, right."

"I'm Jon."

Sarah almost laughed out loud. Of course, he was Jon! Everybody knew Jon Pearce!

"Please to meet you, Mr. Pearce."

"No, no. Please call me Jon. No need for formalities between musicians."

"Okay." Sarah blushed, thrilled that he put her in the same category as himself.

"You're the first to audition. The guy before you

had to cancel. Emergency dental appointment, I think." He shrugged and smiled. His easy manner won Sarah's confidence immediately.

"Wow! Are you going to play a concerto?" he pointed to the pile of music she carried.

"No," she giggled. "Just a little Beethoven and my favorite Carole King song."

"Sounds pretty good. Shall we get started?"

"Sure."

They went to the piano and Sarah set up her music for "Für Elise" while Jon took a seat to the side and somewhat behind her.

"Boy, was this piano ever a mess," Jon commented. "You'll be glad to know we had it tuned this week so no one would have to audition with a handicap."

"I guess it was in pretty poor shape. I don't think anyone's touched it in years," Sarah added.

"It's a real shame, too. I love old pianos like this. They're like friends you write songs with. This one reminds me of a grandmother."

"What do you mean?"

"Well, it's old and sort of fat and very funky. Can't you just see a bunch of little kids sitting in this piano's lap, learning how to sing? You know what I mean?"

Sarah leaned back and considered the piano. "I think you're right. It's beautiful."

"Well, if grandma's ready you can start."

"Right. I'll start with my Beethoven piece—'Für Elise.'"

Jon nodded encouragingly. The instrument's action was somewhat different from her piano at home, and the difference threw Sarah off for a moment. But as she continued to play, she came to like the piano's sound and feel. The sweet lilting melody emanated from it like sunshine. The composition sounded even better than she remembered it. As she took the first repeat, she thought of Jon's comparing the old piano to a grandmother. A grandmother named Elise, she mused. Yes, of course, the melody was the perfect theme song for a kindly old woman with rosy cheeks, snow white hair, and a canary's soprano. As the image of Grandmother Elise became clearer in her mind, Sarah's performance took on a gently nostalgic feel, an infectious warmth.

As the last chord of the piece faded, Sarah slowly turned toward Jon for the verdict.

He was smiling. "Very nice, Sarah. Very nice."

"Thanks."

"Please, go on."

"Okay. Now I'm going to play 'You've Got a Friend.'"

Again he nodded reassuringly.

As she began the familiar tune, repeating her usual accents and embellishments, her thoughts drifted back to the last time she'd been in the music room. The peach-colored walls and the dark-stained woodwork were just as she remembered them from when she was a freshman, rehearsing with the disastrous attempt at a Maplewood High Choral Society.

They had sounded like a pack of alley cats assisted by a few stray hounds in the bass section. Steve was one of the basses—a perfectly awful voice.

Thinking of Steve, she stumbled over a few notes, but quickly recovered. She was annoyed with herself for letting Steve bother her again—and during her audition of all times! But now that she was thinking about him, she couldn't stop, and once again her longing for him affected her playing. She was unaware of the melancholy, pleading tone she was putting into "You've Got a Friend."

Finishing up the last notes of the song, Sarah bent her head for a second, then forced a smile and turned around toward Jon.

"That was lovely. I've never heard 'You've Got a Friend' played like that before."

"Ah . . . thank you . . . I think." Sarah wasn't sure whether he meant it was good or bad.

"No, I mean it. Your interpretation is very touching. I guess I never thought of it as a sad song. You know, usually it's sung as if one person was offering her friendship, probably her love, to another. But your interpretation is more like longtime lovers about to break up and one person is trying to keep it together. That really gives the song a unique twist. I think it's great."

Sarah shrugged, embarrassed. "Thanks," she murmured, all the while dying inside with the fear that her innermost emotions were becoming evident to the world.

"Well, now that I can see you can play, let's see if you can teach," Jon said cheerily, changing the mood. "Suppose I were your piano student and this was my first lesson. How would you start to teach me?"

"Well, first I'd find out whether you could read music."

"Okay, let's suppose I can't."

"All right." Sarah reached on top of the piano and took down one of her beginner piano books. She opened the first page where a line of music was printed with all the different notes displayed.

"I would start off by showing you where all the notes are—what notes are on the lines and what notes are in the spaces. Then I'd explain about the clefs, time signatures, sharps, flats, naturals, major and minor keys, note values and so on. In fact, I'd probably spend the entire first lesson just teaching you how to read music."

"Okay. Now let's say I had my first lesson and I went home and studied up all week. Now I'm back for my second lesson. What will you do?"

"Let's see . . . well, first I'd make sure you could read music and match the notes on the scales with the keys on the piano correctly. Then I'd show you some basic fingering so that you could go home and practice the C-scales."

"Okay, now I've done all that and it's my third lesson."

"Now I'd figure that you were probably getting pretty bored with all these preliminaries, so I'd get the simplest piece of music I could find—probably 'Twinkle, Twinkle, Little Star'—and I'd get you started on that just so you could see that all your work really does lead up to playing a melody. At the same time, we'd proceed with the beginner's book, practicing more and more scales, building up your musical skills and knowledge each week."

"How about homework? Would you assign any?"

"Oh, yes. I'd assign specific scales and exercises, and if you didn't play them well the next week, I'd assign them again. And we'd stay with it until you got it right no matter how long it took."

"Good."

"I had a pretty strict piano teacher. I know I would have never learned a thing if she hadn't been tough. That's why I'd be strict, too."

"It certainly sounds as though you've given the problems of teaching some thought. I'm glad to hear it."

Sarah smiled smugly despite herself. So far it seemed that her strategy might pay off. Jon opened a spiral notebook and wrote something down. She had no doubt that he was taking notes on her.

"Obviously I can't tell you now if you're in or not, Sarah. You're the first to audition and I have eight more pianists to hear. However, I can tell you that I'll be picking four piano teachers, and I will do my best to have made my selections by Monday. The list of music teachers will be posted outside the principal's office. Okay?"

"Okay."

"Thanks a lot for coming. I enjoyed hearing you play." He sounded as though he meant it.

"Thanks." An hour ago he was Jon Pearce the big

rock star to Sarah, but now he seemed like a good friend. "Bye now."

"So long, Sarah. See you around."

As Sarah left the music room, feeling very good about the audition, she almost walked into the next candidate who was standing in the doorway with his guitar case resting on his foot.

"Oh, excuse me—" Then she looked up. It was Bernard.

"I'm so sorry. I was in the way." His voice was a husky whisper. Quickly he stepped aside.

"No, I wasn't looking where I was going." Sarah wanted to leave immediately, but she also wanted to linger.

"You play very well," he commented. "I hope you don't mind that I listened."

"Oh, no. Thank you."

He nodded politely with a shy smile and then entered the music room.

Out in the hallway, Sarah's heart was pounding as she leaned up against the cool walls and listened to Bernard introduce himself to Jon. She felt like a spy, eavesdropping like this, but she couldn't bring herself to leave. She overheard Bernard say that he was going to play Tarrega's "Adelita" first. Sarah had never heard of it before, but she fell in love with it at once. The melody that emerged from that room was romantic. It was a song that went with big pale moons and candlelight and gypsies. The more she heard, the more she wanted to stay and listen.

But suddenly she realized that there was a good

chance that Lisa Forster might show up to meet her new boyfriend. Sarah didn't want to get caught listening like this, especially not by Lisa. Quietly she rushed down the hall on the balls of her feet, the sweet guitar notes diminishing behind her. On the third floor, she realized she was very short of breath. To compose herself, she deliberately walked calmly the rest of the way down the stairs. From just looking at her, no one could tell that the melody of "Adelita" was playing in her mind.

9

There it was! She knew it. After checking that bulletin board countless times all day, Sarah knew every flyer, notice and poster by heart, so even from this far away she could tell that something new had been tacked up. It *had* to be Jon's list of those chosen for the music school. He promised he'd have it up by Monday. She approached the list with more than a little anxiety.

Holding her breath, she read down the list.

PIANO: Dunbar, Paul
                                  Goldman, Naomi
                                    Jordan, Sarah
                                    Lane, Barbara

She bit her lower lip, but she still couldn't suppress her grin. All weekend she had been dreading the possibility that she would not be picked. She and Jon had gotten along so well at the audition, she couldn't imagine not being part of the music school. She had found herself thinking about the music school frequently these days, fantasizing about the responsibilities of being a teacher and the joys of being part of a select group of fellow teachers. She had even imagined a group photograph of all the music teachers with Jon and Ms. Stillman. That's how badly she wanted to belong to the music school. Curious to see who else would be in her imaginary group portrait, Sarah perused the rest of the list.

TRUMPET:	Barry, Christopher
	Lemire, Joseph
SAX:	Clere, Douglas
FLUTE:	Dugan, Pat
TROMBONE:	Latimore, Walter
VIOLIN:	Browne, Fran
	Konig, Eve
DRUMS:	Ryan, Gary
GUITAR:	Altman, Bill
	Curtis, Melissa
	Nobile, James
	St. Onge, Bernard
	Tanner, Mike
	Wright, Linda

Thank heavens, Gary made it! Sarah sighed with relief. *I don't know what he would have done if he hadn't,* she thought.

Then she stared at Bernard's name for a long moment, recalling the sweet melody of the piece he played for his audition. "Adelita"—she wouldn't forget it. Too bad he had had to go for Lisa. He seems like such a nice guy.

Sarah's sigh echoed lightly through the empty hallway. She found a pen in her bag and wrote down the details of the next music school meeting—Wednesday at three o'clock in the music room—then turned and slowly wandered out of the building.

She pushed through the crash bar of the heavy front door. It swung closed behind her with a boom that resounded loudly through the tranquil hallway. In the wake of that noise, Lisa Forster descended the stairs from the second floor in her usual mannered way, as if she were making her formal entrance at a debutante ball. She stopped at the bulletin board and casually glanced at the various announcements with half-closed eyes. Then she spotted Jon's list of music school teachers. Her eyes widened as she ran her long, coral fingernail down the list, scratching a deep vertical crease through the names. Stopping at Bernard's name, she underlined it repeatedly with her pointy fingernail.

"Super, Bernie dahling," she whispered to herself. She grinned, then sauntered down the hall with a confident step.

"Okay, can I have your attention please?" Kathy Stillman tried to override the buoyant chatter of the excited group gathered in the music room. "I'd like to get started if everyone is here."

Gradually the talk subsided.

"First off, I want to congratulate all of you for passing your auditions. Jon said that all the candidates were impressive, but you people were the cream of the crop."

"Jon won't be here today," Ms. Stillman continued. "He had some pressing business. So I thought I'd talk to you about your responsibilities as music school teachers. Your first responsibility, of course, is your student. You're obligated to teach him or her the basics of your instrument, and you will be expected to give your undivided attention and your very best efforts to that task. I know all of you, and I don't think any of you would have auditioned if you weren't committed to this project. So that won't be a problem. Right, Gary?"

Gary Ryan had been caught gazing out the window, lost in a daydream. "Huh? Yeah . . . right, Ms. Stillman."

"Glad to have you back, Gary," she quipped, shaking her head. "Now your other responsibility," she continued, "is to the music school in general— that is, to the operation and maintenance of the business. Mrs. Graham has allotted a loan of $100 to get us started, but that's not much and we won't last long on it. Keep in mind that we're working for fun and profit, so don't forget to collect your tuition fees from your students. It'll cost them $3 per one-hour lesson, and you're responsible for collecting it. Try not to let them get behind in their tuition payments, and if possible, see if you can get them to pay for a few lessons in advance. We're going to have a lot of expenses at first—for ledgers, music books, letterhead, and other miscellaneous supplies. Furthermore, we have to pay rent on this room—$80 a month, payable to the principal's office on the first of every month. And just like any other landlord, you only get a five-day grace period to come up with the rent.

"If you think you're going to need any other supplies—special notebooks, guitar picks, saxophone reeds, metronomes, whatever—please let me know this week in a written request so that at the next meeting we can divvy up our budget properly and decide what items can wait until we start showing some profits.

"I won't get into the matter of setting up a ledger and keeping books today. After you've each given your first lesson, we'll have another meeting where I'll discuss all that. It'll make much more sense to you if I explain how to keep books after we've really gotten underway. You'll understand the need for it then."

She stopped for a moment and put her hands on her hips. "You're too quiet. You should have questions. Or do I talk too much?" She smiled warmly.

Paul Dunbar raised his hand. "What we want to know is when do we get our students so we can start teaching?"

"I was just about to get to that, Paul. As you know, your pupils will be eleven- and twelve-year-olds from Jefferson Junior High. When Jon went over to Jefferson to recruit students, the response was overwhelming. As you can imagine, Jon himself was the best advertisement any music school could ever have. As a matter of fact, we now have a waiting list in case we decide to take on more pupils later. Anyway, I've mimeographed this list for you." She picked up a pack of papers and started to pass them out. "As you'll see, your student's name will be next to yours, along with the days and times that he or she will be available for lessons. It'll be up to you to arrange the time for your lessons, but please try to be flexible. Unfortunately we only have this room, which means that only one lesson can be given at a time."

"I can't believe it!" Gary whispered out loud as he stared at the list. "I've got a girl! A girl playing drums? You've got to be kidding!"

Sarah's student was named Joseph Blake. What is he like? she wondered. Is he a stuffy little Joseph, a cute little Joey, or just a plain Joe? She couldn't wait to meet him.

"All right. We can start with lessons as soon as late next week. But first Jon wants each of you to make up a four-week lesson plan. If you can get those to me by the end of this week, Jon will go over them this weekend. After he approves your lesson plans, you can then call your students and make arrangements for your first lessons."

The music teachers were buzzing with excitement as they could see their school beginning to take shape.

"Now just a few more words and I'll let you go. When you write up your lesson plans, keep in mind that each weekly lesson should be about an hour long. Your lesson plans don't have to be long and elaborate, however. No more than one typewritten page for each week. Just give a general idea of what you plan to do, what your objective for each week will be, and what homework you will assign. And again, please get them to me by Friday morning so we can get started." By the time Ms. Stillman finished, the eighteen music teachers were chattering out loud, excited with their students and their upcoming lessons.

Only Sarah and Bernard remained seated, quietly regarding the names of their individual pupils. They were oblivious to the chaos around them.

Sarah was dying to know what Joseph Blake was like and began piecing together several different imaginary eleven-year-old boys in her mind. *My first student, my little Mozart,* she thought proudly.

A week and a half later, Sarah sat at the old piano in the music room, playing random chords. It was ten minutes after three on Friday afternoon, and the fourth floor was empty except for Sarah. Joseph Blake was late for his first lesson, and Sarah was concerned. What a disappointment it would be if he didn't show up after all her planning and anticipating!

Probably stuck in traffic or something, she told herself. After all, Mrs. Blake assured her on the phone that she'd bring him over to the high school herself.

She continued to play chords to pass the time, then lapsed into "You've Got a Friend" when suddenly she was startled by an odd sound. It was like the stuttering of a baritone Donald Duck.

"Hi. You must be Sarah. I'm Joey." The strange croaking was so rapid-fire only the depth of his voice kept him from being totally incomprehensible.

Sarah spun around on the piano bench. She was speechless. There was Joey Blake—short and wiry with a shock of curly black hair, glinting black-diamond eyes, a petulant pout for a mouth, and a great rip in the knee of his jeans. Some little Mozart! she sighed to herself before she could manage a greeting.

"Ah . . . hi, Joey. Glad to meet you. I'm Sarah."

"Yeah, I know. I just said that."

"So . . . why don't you sit down and tell me about yourself?" Sarah indicated a nearby desk.

"Oh, I thought I was gonna get a lesson."

"Well, you are, Joey. I just thought we'd get acquainted."

"Why can't I sit at the piano? This is a piano lesson, right?"

"Sure, you can if you like." Sarah made room on

the bench, not wanting to antagonize Joey at the start.

Joey hopped up on the bench and cracked his knuckles loudly. "Okay, what do I do first?"

"Well, first we talk." Sarah shut the lid over the piano keys. She was beginning to get annoyed.

"I don't want to talk," he boldly opened the lid, "I want to play, man."

"Can you read music?"

"Naw."

"Well, how do you expect to play if you can't read music?"

"Don't need to."

"How do you know?"

"Aw, come on. You don't have to read music to play rock 'n' roll. Everybody knows that. I mean, you aren't gonna try an' teach me all that classical stuff, are you?" He said "classical stuff" with the same disparaging tone that he probably used for words like *homework, take out the garbage* and *liver*.

"But reading music is essential to playing all kinds of music." Sarah was almost gritting her teeth by now.

"Believe me, readin' music is a waste. I mean, guys like Billy Joel don't read music. That's what I want. To play just like Billy Joel!" He started to gyrate, shaking his head like a little rock robot.

"But, Joey, you have to learn the basics of music before you can play anything. I want to begin by showing you where the notes are on the page and then comparing them to where they are on the piano."

"I know where the notes are. Look, I'll show you." He then attacked the piano with three fingers, banging out a merciless, ragged three-chord blues progression.

Sarah winced. This shouldn't be happening to Grandmother Elise.

"See. I can't read music and I figured that out all by myself." He folded his arms over his chest and grinned smugly.

"Well . . . it's good . . . as far as it goes."

"What does that mean?" Joey was insulted.

"It means that you'll never get much farther than that if you don't learn the basics."

"You don't understand," he grimaced. "Aren't there any teachers around here who'll teach just rock? That's all I want."

"Joey, it's *you* who doesn't understand. You can't—"

Suddenly there was a gentle knock at the door and Jon Pearce poked his head in. "Hi, Sarah. How's it going?"

Joey nearly fell off his seat. His tiny eyes widened and his jaw dropped. *"Jon Pearce!"* he whispered in awe. "Wow!"

"Not so good, Jon. This is Joey Blake. He doesn't think it's necessary to learn how to read music."

"Oh, I see." Jon rubbed his chin. "Why don't you want to read music, Joey?"

"Well, ah . . . I want to play rock. You know, like you and the Makers."

"Ah-hah . . ." Jon's tone was noncommittal.

108

"Well, I thought you didn't need all that stuff to play rock."

"No?"

"I mean, I just want to play like Billy Joel. You know what I mean?"

"You've got some pretty weird notions about rock, Joey. I read music. So do all the guys in the Makers. In fact, there wouldn't have been any Makers at all if we hadn't all studied music formally."

"Oh . . . well, what about Billy Joel? He just learned on his own, didn't he?" Jon Pearce's presence had transformed Joey's voice into a high-pitched squeak.

"Hardly. I know for a fact that he took lessons for almost ten years. Classical lessons, too. Very strict training."

"Really?" Joey's voice was barely audible now.

"Yessir. I've heard him play Bach and Beethoven myself. He's such an accomplished pianist he can do variations on a Mozart sonata, say, pick up the beat, and gradually get into 'Just the Way You Are.' You can't do that unless you really know your stuff."

"Oh. . . ."

"You don't really think he learned to play that well without some kind of training, do you?"

"No, I guess not."

"If you're serious about playing, you'll listen to Sarah. Believe me, she wouldn't steer you wrong. It's up to you, of course. But if I were in your shoes, I'd stick it out with Sarah for a while. I mean, nothing worthwhile is ever accomplished without a little patience and a lot of diligence."

"Right." Joey seemed convinced.

"Well, I've got to be on my way," Jon started for the door. "Have a nice weekend, Sarah. And good luck, Joey. It was nice meeting you."

"You too! So long." Joey's chatter was back up to 78 rpms.

"Take it easy, Jon," Sarah said as Jon closed the door behind him.

"Okay," Joey blurted out, pointing at Grandmother Elise's keys, "let's get started."

10

The phone rang twice. Mrs. Jordan picked it up in the den.

"Hello?"

"Hello? Mrs. Jordan? This is Penny."

"Hi, Penny. How *are* you? It seems as though I haven't seen you in weeks."

"Busy, Mrs. Jordan," Penny said cheerily. "The Junior Professionals' Theater takes up most of my free time."

"Yes, Sarah's music school keeps her pretty busy, too."

"Is she there, Mrs. Jordan?"

"Sure. Hold on, I'll get her."

Mrs. Jordan set down the receiver, then went to the hallway to call up to Sarah. "Telephone, Sarah. It's Penny."

Lifting her head from her math book, Sarah yelled back from her room. "Thanks, Mom. I'll take it up here in your bedroom."

"Fine."

Sarah dashed into her parents' bedroom where the setting sun could be seen peeking through the amber and brown leaves shifting in the autumn breeze. She picked up the receiver and plopped herself down on the edge of the big bed.

"Hello, Penny?"

"Hi."

"What's up?"

"I'm going to the mall tonight to look for a winter jacket. You want to come?"

"Gee, I'd like to, but I've got a lot of work to do."

"Do it tomorrow."

"Can't."

"Come on, Sarah. We haven't gone shopping in over a month. It seems as though we hardly see each other at all anymore."

"Well, that's only because we've been so involved in the Junior Professionals' thing. Between my giving lessons and working on the music school books, and your running around to rent films, it's no wonder we never seem to get together."

"Yeah," Penny said with a note of regret. "I hardly see Gary either. Always preparing his lessons, he says."

"How's he getting along with his pupil? He was pretty bummed out when he found out he'd be teaching drums to a girl."

"That's all changed. Barbara—that's her name—she looks like butter wouldn't melt in her mouth. But when she gets behind her drum set, she goes crazy. Gary's always raving about how good she is and how fast she learns. Sometimes I feel like I'm being jilted for an eleven-year-old."

"I doubt it."

"Why?"

"Nobody but you could put up with Gary's weirdness."

"Thanks a lot! And how's your little brat doing?"

"Joey? Incredible. He's still a brat, but he's incredible. I swear he must do nothing but practice. He's such a smart little guy, I have to double up on his lessons now. In fact I try to pile the work on him to slow him down, but every week he comes back and he knows his exercises perfectly. I've never seen a kid like him."

"Is he still a wise guy?"

"More than ever. Keeps saying he'll give me a couple of pointers on rock sometime. And the worst part about it is that I'm really getting to like the little jerk. My little Mozart."

"What?"

"That's what I call him when he gets wise—my little Mozart. He hates it. All he's really interested in is playing like Billy Joel."

"Hey, that reminds me. Are you going to the Billy Joel concert?"

"I want to, but I haven't asked my parents yet."

"Boy, do I envy you guys in the music school! Free tickets to the Makers/Billy Joel concert at Madison Square Garden. It's not fair! Mr. Rizzo isn't taking the theater workers anywhere."

"I see Gary must have told you all about it. Jon's treating us to the concert to show his appreciation for all the work we're putting into the music school. I heard that he's even paying for a charter bus out of his own pocket."

"You know what kills me, though?"

"What?"

"For once Gary is all excited about going to a decent concert—I mean a concert that *I* would like—and I can't go. Geez! Wanna bet the next time he picks a concert it'll be somebody like the Asthmatics or Repro?"

"Knowing Gary, you're probably right. By the way, did he mention the recital to you?"

"No, what recital?"

"The one the music school is putting on in December."

"No, he didn't tell me anything about it. It figures. Gary never remembers to tell me about the good stuff."

"All the students and teachers of the music school are putting on a show. Joey and Barbara are going to be part of a student rock group. That should be a riot. I think Gary and Paul Dunbar and a couple of other guys are putting together a group for the occasion, too. The plan is to sell enough tickets to increase our budget so we can keep the music school going through the spring. We'd like to expand after Christmas break. If we make enough money at the box office, we can rent another room and take on more students.''

"Sounds pretty good. What are you going to do for the recital?"

"I don't know yet. Ms. Stillman wanted me to play a piano duet with Naomi Goldman. I told her no way, I could never keep up. I'm not too keen on playing a solo piece either. Maybe I'll ask Pat Dugan if she'd like to work up some piano and flute duet." Sarah sat back on the bed and fiddled with the telephone cord as she talked.

"Why don't you team up with a couple of the guitarists and form another group? I'm sure Gary would love to play drums in *two* groups."

"I thought of that, but most of the guitar teachers have already made plans. The only one available is Bernard."

"So why don't you team up with him?"

Sarah sat up suddenly. "Ah . . . I don't know. Anyway he doesn't have an electric guitar. A piano would just drown him out on stage."

"Oh. . . ."

"Yeah." Sarah wound the telephone cord tightly around her finger.

"You know, speaking of Bernard, I overheard the preppy queen going on about him to her little group of disciples in the locker room today."

"Oh, yeah."

"Yeah. Get this! She said she was going to get Bernard to take her to the Winter Carnival Ball."

"I thought she already had something going with him."

"Only in her mind."

"But what about the time we saw them together at the mall."

"From what I overheard today, I gather that she only ran into him that Saturday. She tried to put the moves on him then, but he wasn't interested. Very shy, she told her buddies."

"Very particular about the company he keeps, I'd say."

"You think he's snobbish?"

"Oh, no, not at all. Just very quiet. Bernard keeps to himself a lot. I guess he still feels awkward at an American high school. Too bad. I heard he's a nice guy when you get him to talk. The guys tell me he plays guitar pretty well, too."

"Have you heard him play?"

"Ah . . . no, I haven't." Sarah suddenly felt embarrassed, offering this much information about Bernard. She decided to play it cool and unconcerned. "It would serve Lisa right if she didn't get a date for the Winter Carnival Ball." This kind of hostility was unusual for Sarah, but Lisa brought out the worst in her.

"Well, we don't have to worry about that—getting dates, I mean."

"*You* don't have to worry about it." Sarah said sadly.

"What about Steve? I thought he was going to make it back for the ball. You two had it all planned, didn't you?"

"We *did.*"

"Oh, no. You mean he still hasn't written to you?"

"Oh, yeah, he wrote. A postcard!"

"That's it? A postcard?"

"Yeah. It was a picture of the campus. He drew an arrow pointing to one of the buildings. On the back he said that was where he lived."

"That's all he said? No other message?"

"Nope. Just 'Love, Steve.'"

"Oh . . ."

"Well, you know how guys are. He'll come around eventually. Gary always does whenever we have a fight."

"Steve's not Gary," Sarah said bluntly. "He never used to be like other guys."

"I wish I could say something encouraging. You sound very upset."

"I guess I am. I'm sorry if I seem to be taking it out on you. It's just that whenever I think about Steve, I just get mad at the whole world. You know what I mean?"

"Yeah, I think I do."

"Well, the Winter Carnival Ball isn't such a big deal. I went last year anyway."

"Come on, Sarah. It's only the beginning of November. The ball is two months off. Something could happen between now and then."

"Like what?"

"Someone might ask you out. You never know. Maybe one of the guys from the music school. Maybe something'll happen at the concert. Those guys don't all have girlfriends."

"Who? Paul Dunbar? He's in love with his piano. Bill Altman is a real space-shot. Walter Latimore is just plain weird—"

"What about Bernard?"

"What about him?" Sarah became defensive.

"He's available. And personally, I'd love to see you ruin Lisa's big plans. What do you think?"

"I think this is a ridiculous conversation. Look, Penny, I'm swamped with work and I want to ask my parents about the concert tonight, too. Besides you'd better get going if you want to go shopping."

"Okay, okay, if that's the—"

"I don't mean to be snippy with you, Penny. You know that. I'm just in a bad mood. Will you meet me for lunch tomorrow? I'll let you know how it went with Mom and Dad."

"Okay. Fifth period in the cafeteria. And I hope you're in a better mood."

"I will be, I promise. See you tomorrow."

"Bye."

Sarah hung up the phone and went to the window. Leaning against the window frame, she stared out at the horizon where the sun was now gone and just a reddish glow remained. The wind rattled the dry leaves on the trees. As she gazed at the creeping twilight, the faces of Steve and Bernard tumbled through her head like a juggler's balls. Then Lisa's face appeared, and everything became totally jumbled. Sarah's temples began to throb. She turned away and went to her room to lie down for a while.

That night after dinner, while Sarah and her parents were still sitting at the table, lingering over coffee and chitchat, Sarah decided the time was right to ask them for permission to go to the concert. She was genuinely worried that they might object. They never really felt it was safe for her to go venturing into the city. And ever since Steve left for college, their fretting over her safety had gradually increased to the point where now they didn't seem to want her to go out at night at all. At least that's how it appeared to Sarah. Still, she was willing to beg for this one because it was a music school activity and she wanted to go very badly.

"Dad?" Her voice was soft and tentative. "Can I ask you something?"

"Sure. What is it?" Mr. Jordan set down his cup.

"Can I go . . . to a concert?"

"Well, I don't know . . . what concert is it?"

"Billy Joel and the Makers."

"The Makers is Jon Pearce's old band, right?"

"Right."

"And who's this other fellow?"

"Billy Joel. He's another rock singer. He's the one who does that song you like, Mom. 'Just the Way You Are.'"

"What one is that, Sarah?" Her mother looked confused.

"You know, the one that starts 'Don't go changin' . . .'?"

"Oh, yes. The ballad. I like that one. At least I can understand the words."

"Well, can I go?"

"Where is it going to be?" Mrs. Jordan asked.

"Madison Square Garden. Jon Pearce is treating all the seniors in the music school. He's even chartering a bus to get us there."

"And how much will this cost?"

"Nothing. Jon's treat. All the way."

"Any chaperones?"

"Jon and Ms. Stillman."

"Who else is going?"

"You know, all the student-teachers in the music school."

"Is Penny going?" Mr. Jordan asked.

"No. She's not in the music school."

"Oh."

"But her boyfriend Gary Ryan is going. You know his father, Dad. He owns Ryan's Hardware Store."

"Sam Ryan? Yes, yes I know him."

Sarah felt they were going around in circles, getting farther and farther from the issue. All she wanted to know was whether she could go or not. This was beginning to sound like a TV quiz show. "Well, what do you think? Can I go?"

"When is this concert?" her mother continued to probe.

"The Friday before Thanksgiving. The twenti-eth."

"Will you be home for dinner?"

"The bus leaves at six-thirty. I guess I could eat quickly before I go."

"You mean this is at night? I just assumed it was a matinee." Her mother seemed surprised.

Sarah prepared herself for the worst. Oh, oh, here we go. Too late. Too dangerous in Manhattan. Really don't think you should go. It's probably easier to get permission to leave Russia than this!

"All rock concerts are at night, Mom. I don't think I've ever heard of one during the day."

"I don't know, dear. . . ."

"Please, Mom. It's a school-sponsored event. There's nothing to worry about."

"Well . . . ask your father."

"Dad? Can I go?" Sarah sounded desperate.

He lifted his cup to his lips and took a sip, savoring her request with his coffee. Slowly he set down his cup, clinking it softly against the saucer. He looked at his wife for a moment, then at Sarah. "Sure. Why not?"

"Really? I can go?"

"I said yes, didn't I?" He smiled warmly at her. "Jon Pearce is an awfully sensible young man. I think he's very trustworthy. And Kathy Stillman will be there, too. I don't think we'll have to worry."

"Thanks, Dad. You're great." She turned to her mother. "You too, Mom. You just worry more." Then Sarah stood up, ready to bolt out of the room. "Excuse me!"

"Hey! Where are you going in such a hurry?"

"Got to figure out what to wear for the concert, Mom. I might have to buy a nice pair of slacks." Instantly she disappeared around the corner and up the stairs.

"This is the girl who is never seen without her jeans?" Sarah's mother asked no one in particular.

Mr. Jordan shrugged and sipped his coffee.

11

On the night of the concert, Mrs. Jordan drove Sarah to school where the mini-bus would be picking everybody up. Stopped at a traffic light, Mrs. Jordan looked over at Sarah and shook her head in amazement, a pleased smile on her face.

"What's the matter, Mom?"

"I just can't get over it."

"What?"

"You! You look so pretty tonight."

"Come on, Mom. This is how I always look."

Mrs. Jordan grinned to herself as the light changed and she drove her faithful green Nova through the intersection.

Sarah was unwilling to admit that she had taken great pains with her appearance tonight. She had bought a pair of lilac dress jeans especially for the occasion. Her top was a lacy, off-white, cable-knit sweater—a beautifully delicate garment that could have come right out of her grandmother's trousseau. With her high-heeled sandals, Sarah's legs looked as long and slender as a model's. Her chestnut brown hair hung loose, gently waved over her shoulders, shimmering with highlights as the car passed under the streetlights. She had used only the barest touch of makeup, just enough to bring out her hazel eyes and embellish her natural good looks. Mrs. Jordan was proud to see her daughter looking so pretty; she was also curious as to Sarah's motives for the big change. She knew better than to ask outright, though.

"There's the bus," Sarah said as they neared the front of the school. Her voice sounded jittery.

"Okay. Now you're sure you don't need a ride back."

"Nope. Gary's got his father's car. He'll take me home. Anyway it'll probably be pretty late. No use you and Dad staying up."

"Okay, just as long as you've got a ride. Have a good time and be careful. After all, you will be in New York."

"Don't worry, Mom. I'll be fine. Bye."

Sarah got out and locked the car door behind her, then waved once more to her mother. However, when she turned and started to walk toward the bus, her heart began to pound. Suddenly she panicked, wondering whether she'd overdressed for the occasion, whether the others would suspect something.

With butterflies in her stomach, Sarah climbed into the small, half-sized bus and faced a bored-looking bus driver who nodded perfunctorily to her. She managed a weak smile, wishing she didn't feel so jumpy. It's only a concert, she kept saying to herself.

"Sarah, you made it." It was Ms. Stillman, sitting up front with Jon Pearce. "I was beginning to wonder if you were coming."

"Am I late?" Had all her primping caused her to hold up the trip?

"Not really. Everyone else decided to come fifteen minutes early."

"Don't worry about it, Sarah," Jon spoke easily. "We still have plenty of time. And we're still waiting for Gary anyway."

"Figures." Sarah shook her head.

"That's a lovely sweater," Kathy complimented her. "May I ask where you got it?"

"This? My grandmother bought it in Ireland when she was there two years ago."

"Well, I must say you're looking very nice tonight," Jon commented. "Very classy."

"Watch it, fella." Kathy elbowed him. "You're a chaperone, remember?"

"Yeah, but I thought I was here to watch you."

"Ha!"

Sarah couldn't believe it, but the way they were kidding around, it certainly looked like Jon and Ms. Stillman had something going together. *Wait'll Penny hears this!* she thought gleefully.

Just then Gary stumbled into the bus, panting and gasping for breath.

125

"Wow! I was afraid I wouldn't make it."

"Catch your breath, Gary. We wouldn't leave without you." Ms. Stillman reassured him. "No matter how late you are."

"Aw, come on, Ms. Stillman. You're always giving me a hard time about being late all the time. I try, but I can't help it."

"I know, Gary. I'm sorry. From now on I'll say you've got 'chronic tardiness.' That way people will think you have an incurable disease and they'll feel sorry for you. Why don't you two find seats so we can get going."

"Right." Gary saluted like a boy scout and raced ahead of Sarah to find a seat.

The bus had just about enough seats for all the music school teachers, Ms. Stillman and Jon. Gary ran straight to the back and wedged himself in between his buddies, Paul Dunbar and Jimmy Nobile. There were only two other seats left—one next to Walter Latimore and one next to Bernard. There was really no choice. She thought about going back up front and sitting with Jon and Ms. Stillman, but then decided against it. They might not want a third wheel. And Walter Latimore was too weird to sit with all the way to Manhattan. So with weak knees, not knowing how he might react, she finally decided to sit next to Bernard. No one could suspect anything when the alternative was Walter Latimore.

"Hi, Bernard." Her voice was embarrassingly squeaky.

"Hello . . . Sarah," he said in his husky whisper.

His shyness was evident from the way he nervously flexed his hands.

Sarah didn't notice his hands, however. It was hearing him say her name that made her heart pound harder. Of course, he knew her name from the music school meetings, but this was the first time she'd ever heard him address her directly. They had said "hi" before, but this was different. It was strange, but very nice.

The bus driver started his engine, and one of the rowdies in the back yelled, "And away we go!" The overwhelming spirit in the bus was jovial. Bernard tried to smile a lot to take part in the silliness even though it was not his style. Eventually the craziness quieted down. When the bus turned onto the highway, the steady hum of the road muffled most of the talk.

All the while, Sarah was dying to think of some topic to discuss with Bernard. He stared out the window and didn't say a word. She wanted to talk to him so badly, but she didn't know what to say that wouldn't sound dumb: Do you like Billy Joel, Bernard? How do you like Maplewood High, Bernard? Nice weather we're having, huh? Each one sounded as bad as the other.

But what if he thinks I'm unfriendly? she thought in dread. *He's going to think I'm stuck up if I don't say something.*

She could feel the sweat gathering on the small of her back as she fretted over what to do. Each time she was on the verge of saying something—anything just to get the conversation started—she'd chicken out, afraid of sounding foolish.

But before she could finally work up the nerve, Naomi Goldman leaned across the aisle and touched her on the arm. "Sarah? Have you decided about the duet for the recital? I'd still like to do it if you're willing."

"Ah . . . I don't know, Naomi. . . ." Sarah's mind was not on the recital or Naomi, her thoughts were riveted on Bernard, who was still staring out the window.

I blew it, Sarah despaired. He must think I don't want to talk to him. I blew it.

The bus pulled up to the curb on the north side of Madison Square Garden, a huge, imposing building that looked like a big grayish brown layer cake. As soon as the bus came to a stop, Jon got up and faced the group.

"Okay, here we are, people. We're on Thirty-third Street. Remember that if any of you get separated, because the bus will be right here after the concert. Now I'm going to give you your tickets." Jon produced a packet of tickets from his pocket. "I couldn't get twenty seats all together so pay attention to your seat numbers. Ten of us will be in the fifth row to the right of the stage, and ten will be in the eighth row in the center section." He began to pass out tickets to everyone in the bus. "Remember, if we lose you, meet back here after the show. And have a good time."

The music teachers got off the bus and entered the Garden together. They climbed flight after flight of steps, and at every turn an usher checked their tickets and directed them to their proper section.

As Sarah expected, there were thousands of people waiting inside, literally an ocean of heads and colorful Billy Joel and Makers T-shirts. Walking down the long aisles, Sarah noticed that several Frisbees were being tossed through the crowd.

It was exhilarating to see such an excited multitude. The air was electric with anticipation. Sarah just wanted to soak it all in, forget about her boy problems and just let herself become part of the crowd.

Unfortunately, Naomi stuck close to her, talking almost nonstop. "Sarah, look! They're playing Frisbee!"

"Yes, they are."

"Well, isn't that against the law or something? I mean throwing it in here?"

"I suppose it could be." Sarah wished she'd go talk to someone else for a while.

Suddenly one of the Frisbees skipped over the outstretched arms in the section near where they were walking and landed in the aisle right in front of Naomi.

Instantly Gary scooped it up and prepared to fling it.

"Wait, Gary!" Sarah said, grabbing his arm. "It hit Naomi's foot. Let her throw it."

"Aw, come on, Sarah. She—"

"Gary!" she stared at him sternly.

"Awright. Here, Naomi, give it a good one for me."

He handed her the Day-Glo orange Frisbee.

"Go ahead, Naomi," Sarah encouraged. "Throw it!"

Giggling wildly, Naomi tossed it into the crowd. The people from Maplewood High along with some of the onlookers in the crowd gave her a rowdy cheer. She blushed beet red.

"We better find our seats, Naomi, before you really get carried away."

"Oh, Sarah, I'm having a great time already!" Naomi's big brown eyes were sparkling behind her wire-frame glasses.

"What's your seat number?"

"Ah . . . EE-14." Naomi clutched her ticket as if she were afraid someone might take it away from her.

"Hmmm . . . mine is HH-102. You're over in the right-hand section. I'm in the center."

"Well, I guess I'll see you later then. Bye." Naomi skipped off to find her seat and Sarah smiled at her departing figure. She had never seen Naomi so slaphappy. She continued down the aisle, looking for row HH. Eight rows from the front, Jon had said. Sarah stopped and counted eight rows back from the stage. Then walking toward her row, she could see from the numbers on the empty seats she passed that the one-o-twos were on the aisle. But when she finally got to row HH, her stomach gave a lurch.

Already sitting in the second seat, right next to her

vacant HH-102, was Bernard. Jon must have passed out the tickets in order on the bus, so naturally they would be sitting together again. Sarah had never thought of that. But now he thinks I'm stuck up because I didn't talk to him on the bus. I'm sure he must! Well, I just can't stand here like a retard or he'll really think I'm a jerk. Sit down, Sarah. And be cool! she admonished herself.

Resolved to rectify any bad impressions she might have made on him, she took a deep breath. "Oh, Bernard! We're sitting together again." As soon as she said it, she felt like a dope.

Politely Bernard stood up as Sarah sat down. His manners were very proper, but very much out of place at a rock concert. Sarah forced a smile, not knowing exactly how to respond to his gesture.

"I have never been to a rock and roll concert before, Sarah," he said softly. "I would appreciate it if you would let me know if I do something out of place."

"Well, ah . . . sure, Bernard." She was trying desperately to be cool. "But there's no code of rules for this kind of thing. You just enjoy yourself."

"Oh . . . all right." He nodded slowly, trying to digest the concept of a social event without strict protocol.

Sarah tried not to look at him too much, but she couldn't help herself. Say something dummy, her brain yelled at her. "Don't worry. I think you'll like this. You know, the Makers—that's the group Jon used to be in—they're on first."

Now she was talking too much and too fast, and

she knew it. Only she didn't know what else to do. Then the houselights went off and the crowd started to cheer.

The cheers increased to a deafening roar as the Makers took the stage. Without any introductions or preliminaries, they ripped into their latest hit, "Far Away."

Bernard seemed to be slightly puzzled but engrossed in the music. Sarah watched his reactions out of the corner of her eye.

The Makers saved their best song for last—"Us," the song that was practically the Maplewood High student anthem. It was an especially exciting rendition with extended solos and extra choruses, and the Maplewood High contingent could be heard singing right along with the choruses. Caught up in the spirit of the concert, Sarah sang too until she suddenly felt embarrassed, afraid of what Bernard might think. She glanced at him out of the corner of her eye again. To her delight, Bernard was as excited as everyone else in the Garden. If he'd known the words, he would have been singing along, too.

The set ended with the Makers taking their bows and demonstrably showing their appreciation for the uproarious adulation. Five minutes later when the cheers began to subside, the houselights were turned on again for intermission.

"That was great!" Bernard declared, turning to Sarah. An unexpected grin made his large eyes shine.

"Did you like it?" She was thrilled and surprised that he had spoken to her first.

"Yes, yes! I've never seen anything like this before. It's so . . . American."

"I'm not sure I know what you mean by that."

"Well, in Belgium I went to many classical concerts—symphonies, string quartets, chamber music. But they were always very proper affairs. People got all dressed up for those concerts, and they sat very quietly so as to listen properly. Very boring, though. You could not always enjoy the music. But here, you can really *feel* the music. I like this very much."

"That's great." She smiled at him.

"Sarah, I'm a bit thirsty. I'm going to get something to drink. May I get you something, too?"

"Yes, will you get me a Coke? Here I'll give you some money—"

"No, no, no. Let me. Please."

"Well, okay . . . sure."

"I'll be right back."

Sarah couldn't believe how nice he was. And all it took was a little rock 'n' roll to loosen him up. *I hope he hurries back*, she thought with a delirious grin on her face.

Unfortunately the lines at the nearest snack bar were so long the intermission was almost over by the time Bernard got back. They had no time to begin another conversation. Just as they were finishing their Cokes, the lights went out and Billy Joel took the stage. His set was even better than the Makers'.

When he left the stage after nearly an hour of

performing, the crowd clapped wildly and stamped their feet for more. The audience wouldn't let him go. A minute later he was back, playing "Only the Good Die Young," and driving his fans crazy. He tried to leave again, but the crowd called him back once more. This time he played "Just the Way You Are," his most popular ballad. ". . . I love you just the way you are," he crooned at the end of every verse.

The bright glare of the spotlight glistened in Sarah's moist eyes. This had been their song—hers and Steve's—and hearing it now brought back all her happy memories of being with him. But each time she heard the refrain—"I love you just the way you are"—her throat got tighter. Steve had changed, and it was painfully clear to her that it would never be the same again. Somehow Billy Joel's live performance of the song made it all too real for her. She had known their relationship was over, but this seemed to confirm it. Before the song was over the tears were flowing down her cheeks, illuminated by the pale white spotlights on stage.

Bernard watched her tears with a worried expression on his face. She didn't notice him, though. She was too consumed with hurt.

On the way home after the concert, Sarah made sure she sat with Bernard again. They spoke easily about the concert now. Having shared an experience, they didn't have to grope for topics of conversation anymore. But although Sarah was buoyant and enthusiastic on the outside, inside she felt empty and washed out.

However, the more they talked, the better she felt. Bernard's polite manner and soft, soothing words made her forget about her troubles with Steve. He talked about his life in Europe and in Chicago after that, and she hung on every word. They spoke so easily, by the time the bus got on the highway, Sarah was wishing he'd ask her out on a real date.

When the mini-bus pulled up in front of Maplewood High shortly after midnight, everyone piled out and said their good-nights. Gary seemed to be in a big hurry, and kept hounding Sarah to hurry up while she tried to say good-night to Bernard.

"Come on, Sarah. Let's go."

"I'll be right there, Gary. Take it easy."

"Aw, come on. I wanna get home and listen to some records. Come on!"

"Go warm up the car. I'll be right there."

"Okay, but if you're not there in two minutes, I'm leavin'."

"Okay, okay, I'm coming—" She turned to Bernard, trying not to look annoyed. "I had a great time, Bernard. I hope you enjoyed it as much as I did."

"Oh, I did, I did. And I want to thank you for your company. You were very nice to me."

"Oh, you don't—"

The blast of a car horn interrupted her. It came from a metallic blue Peugeot station wagon.

"There is my father, Sarah. I must go now. Thank you again. You are . . . *très gentille*." He took her hand in both of his and shook it gently.

Later that night, Sarah lay in bed wide awake, thinking about Bernard. Her hand was still tingling where he'd touched her.

12

The next week was a short one because Thursday was Thanksgiving Day. The general mood around Maplewood High was up, since everyone was looking forward to the four-day weekend. Even the tough teachers seemed to lighten up during Thanksgiving week. Thanksgiving also always seemed to signal the beginning of winter and all the big school events that led up to Christmas, particularly the Winter Carnival. And this year the music school teachers had something extra to look forward to—their recital. But while everyone in school seemed to be buzzing about one upcoming event or another, Sarah was thinking about Bernard.

All through the weekend after the concert, she had been walking on clouds, thinking about him, about dates with him, about going places with him, about playing duets with him, about going steady with him. On Monday morning she was happier than she had been in months, full of hopes and dreams. But when she got to school, her dreams began to sour the instant she spotted Lisa Forster in the hallway.

Sarah had wanted to make her feelings known to Bernard very badly. After the night of the concert, she was sure she would be his choice over Lisa. But she couldn't make her feelings known, not yet. She and Steve had to talk first. The thought of confronting Steve filled her with dread. By Wednesday she was totally consumed with Steve all over again. Her feelings for him were so confused she didn't want to deal with him at all. But she would have to and soon. Tomorrow was Thanksgiving. He would surely be home for the holiday.

Since August he'd only written two postcards and a very short letter. What a letdown that letter had been. After diligently checking the mail for weeks and weeks, she had immediately ripped the letter open with trembling fingers, all her hopes suddenly renewed. Then she read it.

Hi,

Just a note to let you know I'm still alive. Classes are getting harder (believe it or not), but I really like it here. We already have snow and we've been out skiing twice. Dorm life is as wild as everyone says—we even had a toga party last week! I'm thinking about pledging for a fraternity. They say the parties are even better in the frats.

I hope everything is going well with your music school. You'll have to introduce me to Jon Pearce sometime.

I have to close now. (Cramming for midterms is a real drag.) Take care.

Love,
Steve

What a jerk! she thought sadly.

He never wrote that he'd be home for Thanksgiving. But he had mentioned it to her at the end of the summer before he left for Cornell. She couldn't forget that.

Still she didn't want to see him. At least not under these circumstances. It had become all too obvious to her that it was over between them, but nevertheless she was afraid to admit it to herself. While he was away, she did get some satisfaction from letting other people believe that they were still together. She never felt totally alone when she thought of herself as Steve's girlfriend, even though she realized she probably wasn't anymore. However, if she confronted Steve and confirmed her fears, she would have to face it—she really was alone.

That thought alone was too devastating for her. Now she couldn't imagine anything beyond their breakup. The notion of vying with Lisa Forster for Bernard now seemed inconceivable.

Thanksgiving dinner was an ordeal for Sarah. She didn't feel like eating at all, but she had to force

139

herself. Her mother always suspected that something was bothering her when she didn't eat, and Sarah wasn't prepared to discuss this problem with her, especially not on a holiday. So Sarah cut her turkey into small shards, hoping that a lot of small bites would create the illusion of a good appetite.

But then there was the phone. Everytime it rang she jumped. And it rang a lot, with friends and relatives calling to wish the Jordans a Happy Thanksgiving. But one of those calls would be Steve, she knew it. When he did call, she'd just have to be as cool as possible. She was tired of being swayed by her emotions. Sarah decided she had to take control.

It was four o'clock and Steve hadn't called yet. The meal was over, and mercifully they had all decided to wait and let their food digest before attempting coffee and dessert. Sarah would never have been able to face pumpkin pie, she felt so nervous and queasy.

As the time dragged on, she got jumpier. She had to talk to someone about it. Thank heavens her brother David was home. There was no one better to share a problem with than David. She pulled him aside and took him out onto the back porch to "get some air."

"What's the matter? You look worried about something." David could always tell whenever something was bothering Sarah.

"Steve. He must be home. But I haven't heard from him yet." Sarah's face was hot and flushed despite the chill November wind.

"Did you try calling him?"

"No, but I did take your advice and I wrote to him first—several times as a matter of fact. Well, all I got back was two lousy postcards and a nothing letter. If he's in town, I think he should call me. If he still cares, that is." There was anger in her eyes.

"Well . . . you may be right," David had to admit. "He may have had a rough first semester, but he could at least call you if he's home."

"Oh, David, I don't know what to do! I feel like I have to do something, but I also feel that I've reached a dead end."

"I know how you feel. But the question is how do you feel about him now? Do you think it will ever be the same between you?"

Sarah looked at the ground, and sighed. "No . . . I don't."

"Why not?"

"Well, I . . . I've thought about us quite a bit. You know, about what it means to have someone —the way you have Marie. And also about what it means to be alone. I felt pretty bad being alone this year, that's why I wrote to him so much and thought about him so much. I think if he felt lonely and missed me too, he would have made a better effort to keep in touch, and of course, you can't keep people from meeting new people—that's just the way things are. If he's got someone else . . . well, there's nothing I can really do about it. And I really can't hate him for that. It's just that he could have done something sooner instead of leaving me hanging like this."

"Maybe he was afraid to."

"What do you mean?"

"Well, let's suppose he did meet someone new and he's made all new friends at Cornell. No one—certainly not Steve—is so callous that he could just cut off one phase of his life to pick up another. Sure, Steve's probably changed, but it's got to be difficult for him because he knows he still has ties to his life in Maplewood. He can't simply ignore the people he knows here. And what if he's not one hundred percent comfortable with his new crowd at Cornell? He may not want to sever all his ties to his past, if you know what I mean."

"Yeah? So how do I fit in?"

"Well, I'd guess that he's still very fond of you, but in a different way. You're part of the past that he's getting away from. But you're also the best part of his Maplewood days, you're the one he probably thinks of when life at Cornell gets weird and high-pressure and he remembers how great things used to be. But everyone wants to move on, and if he thinks of you as part of the past he's trying to grow out of, he's really torn."

"You mean, it's not me personally as much as what I represent to him."

"Exactly."

"All right. I guess I can understand that, but I'm still afraid to see him. If it's over, I don't want to have a scene. I'd rather just get a letter in the mail, like a college rejection."

"Ha! Life should be so easy."

"Isn't there any easier way to do this? Why do I feel like crawling under the blankets?"

"I wish I had a good answer for—"

"Sarah?" Mr. Jordan suddenly poked his head out of the storm door. "Telephone."

"Who is it, Dad?" She immediately felt nauseated.

"Steve Dowd."

"Ah . . . tell him . . . I'll be right there." Sarah looked frantic.

David put his arm around her shoulder and led her into the house. "Come on," he whispered. "I'll bet he's as scared as you are. Maybe more."

Their conversation was short, almost formal. He asked if he could come over to show her his new Jeep. Reluctantly, she agreed. He said he'd be right over. All through the conversation, Sarah had had stomach cramps, and as she sat by the window in her room overlooking the front yard, she could feel her Thanksgiving dinner roiling around inside her like an evil spirit.

When the sparkling new, coffee-brown Jeep pulled up in front of the house, her heart started to palpitate and her hands were shaking. For a moment, she wanted to disappear, but then she saw him getting out of the Jeep. He looked the same, but something about him was different. Not having seen him in all these months Sarah felt that he seemed more like a stranger. She was surprised by her feelings, very surprised.

She watched out the window as David walked down the flagstone walk to greet Steve. They shook hands. Steve started showing off his Jeep and David just stood with his hands in his jacket pockets, nodding agreeably. Steve was bouncing all over his new toy, pointing out its features while practically tripping over his own feet, his open jacket flapping behind him. He was usually more together than this, Sarah recalled. His hair was longer, a wild tangle of halfhearted curls. By comparison, David looked so much older, and yet he was only a year ahead of Steve.

All of a sudden the thought of facing Steve was not quite so awesome. Her stomach cramps were gone and so were her shakes. Calmly she stood up, walked downstairs, put on her down jacket, and went outside. It was time to face the music.

When Steve spotted Sarah coming down the walk, he seemed very nervous. He looked at her, then at David, then at his Jeep. Finally when she was at the edge of the flagstone walk, he approached her awkwardly. "Sarah, how've you been?" he asked. Hesitating for a split second, he threw his arms around her and gave her a bear hug. She returned the hug, but neither seemed to want to attempt a kiss.

"Hi, Steve," Sarah said evenly. "What's new?"

"Ah . . . *this!*" He pointed to his Jeep, looking like some dumb husband in a car commercial on TV. "I was just telling David all about it. Great pickup! Four-wheel drive, AM-FM stereo, everything. Hey, wanna take a ride? Come on, you too, David."

"No thanks, Steve," David smiled kindly. "I've got a few phone calls to make. But you two go ahead. I'm sure you've got a lot to talk about."

"You sure? We won't be long." Steve seemed anxious to have David go along with them.

"No thanks. Some other time, Steve."

"Okay, maybe some other time. . . ." He was stalling, Sarah was certain.

"Come on, Steve. Let's go," she finally said, letting herself into the Jeep.

Obediently, he ran around and got into the driver's seat.

As Steve started the engine and slowly pulled away from the curb, David nodded to her encouragingly and gave her the thumbs up sign.

Thinking it was for him, Steve waved back to David.

But Sarah knew better.

As he wound through the streets of Maplewood, driving too fast, Steve jabbered on and on about college, his dorm, his new buddies and his classes. He talked nonstop, something he never used to do. It was as if he were trying to keep her from saying anything. But Sarah had just one question she wanted to ask him, and she was willing to wait patiently for him to run out of steam so she could ask it.

"Ah . . . so . . . would you like to try?" He indicated the steering wheel. "Try it, Sarah. It drives easy, just like a car."

She knew he must have finally run out of things to say. Unless he'd forgotten that she didn't know how to drive a manual transmission.

"I can't drive a stick shift. Remember?"

"Oh, yeah. Well, I thought maybe you might have learned this fall or something."

"No."

"Oh. . . ."

The pauses were becoming longer and more embarrassing.

"Steve? Can I ask you a question?" She stared straight ahead, her eyes glued to the road.

"Sure . . . what?"

"Why didn't you write to me while you were away?"

"I did write, Sarah. I sent you postcards and stuff."

"Two postcards and a note."

"Right."

"Steve, I must have written you twenty times since you left. Don't you think you could have written me one real letter? Or maybe called?"

"Well, ah . . . I was busy, Sarah. Classes are a real grind, and I spend almost every night in the library. . . . You know how it is?"

"No, Steve . . . I don't think I do." She had the jitters again.

Steve pulled the Jeep over to the curb and cut the engine. His hands remained gripped on the wheel as he tried to look her in the eye.

"Sarah . . . I never meant to hurt you or anything, but . . . I . . . I think we should have a break in the action. I think we should . . . maybe date other people for a while."

"Why?" Her stomach cramps were back.

"Well"—he was breathing heavily now—"you're

here and I'm up there, and we never get to see each other anymore. I mean, I thought about you a lot and I really missed you. But there was a lot of stuff going on up at school, and you just can't sit around your room and not participate."

"You mean you're going out with someone up there?"

"Well, no. Not exactly. I mean I've met new people—some girls, too. And there's one who—"

"I understand, Steve," she interrupted. She didn't want to hear the details. "I think you're probably right. A relationship is no good unless you can be together. We probably do need a break in the action—even if it's just for a while." Sarah listened to her own words as if it were someone else talking.

Then there was a long silence. Insulated in the new Jeep, the only sounds they could hear were of their own breathing. Finally Steve reached over and took her hand.

"You're not mad, are you?" He could barely talk he was so choked up.

"No," she whispered, "no one's to blame. It just happens this way sometimes." She glanced over at him, and his eyes were pleading. He looked as though he really wanted to embrace her, to do something, anything to repair the damage.

Sarah reached for the door handle and threw the door open. "Steve . . . I want you to know that I'm not mad at you. Really. Maybe we can talk more later, after we've thought about it. But right now, I just want to be alone."

"Well, close the door. I'll take you home."

"No, I'd rather walk. I need to think."

"Okay . . . if that's what you want. . . ."

"Yes."

"I'll be in touch, I promise."

"Fine. Take care, Steve. Good luck at school."

"Bye."

She shut the door behind her and just started walking. She didn't want to look back. When she got to the end of the block, she finally heard Steve start his engine in the distance.

The sky was gray, and streetlights were already beginning to flicker on. It was cold, and a thin wind whistled through the bare trees.

Sarah just walked and walked, heading vaguely for home. Her head throbbed as thoughts and memories hurtled through her mind. Only one thing was clear to her, however. It was over. There wouldn't be anymore discussions or letters or anything. It was over. The next time she saw him, they would be like acquaintances. No, like best friends from grammar school who'd drifted apart a long time ago.

She couldn't blame him, though. David was right, she told herself. Things just happen this way. People change. That's all. It's not as if I didn't expect it. It hurts now, but it won't always hurt. I hope.

13

She didn't tell anyone. Not even Penny. Only David knew because he had seen it coming from the way Steve had acted on Thanksgiving. Afterward, David told Sarah that when they were standing around together before she came down, Steve had been straining to make conversation with him, trying to get him to stick around so that he wouldn't have to face her alone and tell her. Sarah confessed that she had suspected that it was over weeks before. He'd never even answered her letters that practically begged him to write back.

"Well, before you completely condemn him, I can assure you that Steve probably feels pretty low right now," David pointed out. "No one can initiate a breakup and not feel very, very guilty."

"I know that," she said. "I don't want him to suffer. That's not what I want."

What she did want, however, was Bernard. Before this she had been unwilling to admit it to herself, but now she knew she had a crush on Bernard. All during that next week, she was preoccupied with the confused state she was in—breaking up with Steve, longing for Bernard, and despairing over the obstacles that stood between her and Bernard. And to make matter worse, the whole school was buzzing about the Winter Carnival, now just three weeks away. She had wanted to go to the Winter Carnival Ball very badly and she had counted on Steve's coming back to take her despite her mixed feelings about him. But I can forget all about that now, she sighed to herself.

Of course, nothing would please her more than going to the ball with Bernard. Everytime she thought of the possibility, she remembered the night of the Billy Joel/Makers concert and how good things had been with him.

If only Lisa Forster would be kidnapped by terrorists. If only Lisa would get on the wrong bus and end up in Siberia. If only Lisa would drop. . . . Sarah wasn't pleased with herself for thinking such things, but she couldn't help it. Lisa was still determined to snag Bernard for the Winter Carnival Ball, everyone knew that. But the way she felt right now—fragile and vulnerable after what she'd been through with Steve—Sarah wasn't sure that she wanted to compete with Lisa for Bernard. She didn't want to risk being hurt again, at least not this soon. Besides, it was no secret that Lisa fought dirty.

For days Sarah racked her brain, trying to decide what to do. And as the time left before the ball dwindled, Sarah began to feel like the helpless maiden tied to the log in the lumber mill just minutes away from the lethal buzz saw. If she was going to do something, she had to do it pretty soon.

By Wednesday, however, she was ready to burst. It was no use trying to keep her problem to herself. She had to talk to someone about it. But who? David was back at school. Penny would get hysterical about the break-up and Sarah wanted to put all that behind her. At lunchtime she sat by herself in the cafeteria, drinking plain tea, distractedly considering other people she could confide in. Ms. Stillman? Jon? Gary? No one seemed to be right. But while Sarah was lost in thought, Naomi Goldman walked up to the table with her lunch tray.

"Sarah?"

"Huh?"

"May I join you for lunch?"

"Ah . . . yeah, sure, Naomi. Sit down." Sarah was momentarily discombobulated.

"Sarah, I wanted to ask you something."

"What's that?"

"Will you reconsider doing a duet with me for the recital?"

Sarah hadn't even thought about the recital since Thanksgiving. She really didn't need anything else to worry about right now. "Gee, Naomi, I don't know.

You play so well I could never keep up with you. Don't you think you'd be better off doing a solo?"

"No, Sarah, that's the whole point. I want to do a duet because I'm tired of being singled out like some great pianist or something. The other kids are having a great time forming groups and trios and duos. I want to do that, too."

Suddenly Sarah came out of her fog. It was clear that she wasn't the only person in the world with a problem. Naomi was practically begging for her friendship, and she had been ignoring her. Sarah was ashamed of herself. "Well . . . I can appreciate your not wanting to do a solo, Naomi. But I really can't think of a decent classical duet that I could play and keep up with you. I'd like to do it, but—"

"Who said anything about a classical piece? I'm willing to play anything, just as long as I don't have to play it alone."

Sarah was moved by her earnestness. "Okay, then," she said after a moment. "We'll do a duet. Do you have anything in mind?"

"How about 'Just the Way You Are.' "

"Ah . . . no . . . I don't think so." With all the memories she associated with that song, there was no way in the world that she could perform it.

"Hmmm . . . Wait a minute! I've got a great idea. Have you ever seen *West Side Story?*"

"Yeah."

"Do you remember the song 'America'?"

"You mean the very fast, Latin number that the Sharks' girls do? 'Everything free in America . . .'?"

"Right! Well, I heard it played for two pianos once and it was great. As a matter of fact, I know one of the guys who played it and he probably still has the arrangement. As I remember, it wasn't very hard. What do you say, Sarah?"

"Hmmm. . . . It is a great song. I tell you what—show me the arrangement and if I think I can do it, we'll start rehearsing right away. Okay?"

"Fantastic! I can get the arrangement tomorrow. The guy who has it lives in Manhattan and I have to go in tomorrow anyway for an interview. I'll show it to you on Friday."

"Great!" Suddenly Sarah felt better than she had in days. "Say, can I ask what the interview is for? I'm nosy."

"It's for school next year. I've applied to a place in France to study piano. The Conservatoire de Paris. It's a really great school, but I've never been to Europe and I'm not sure I'd like to be so far from home for so long. Have you ever been to France?"

"No, I haven't, but . . ." Sarah's words trailed off as she suddenly thought of something else. A hopeful grin appeared on her face as she started to nod to herself.

"Sarah? Are you there? What's the matter?"

"Thanks, Naomi, you've just given me an idea."

"Huh? What are you talking about?"

"Let's just say I think you may have solved more than just the problem of the recital for me."

That afternoon after last period, Penny and Gary ran into Sarah rushing down the hallway toward her locker.

"Hey, Sarah, what's the big hurry?" Penny smiled, stepping into her path.

"Ah . . . I have to see someone." She tried to get past Penny.

"Hang on a minute! You got time for a trip to Burger King? Gary's buying."

"I am! Says who?" Gary glared down at her, clenching his gangly hands and trying to appear angry.

"Says me, Gary," Penny said. "What do you say, Sarah? Coming?"

"Sorry, Penny. I really can't today. This is important."

"So what's so urgent?"

"Ah . . . dentist appointment. You know, if you're late, they make you pay for the time anyway."

"They do? Mine doesn't."

"Mine does. Sorry, I've got to run. Bye!"

Then she dashed off, weaving in and out of the groups of kids congregating in the hallway.

"Sarah? Is that you?" Mrs. Jordan's voice wafted into the hallway from the kitchen.

"Yes, Mom." She walked through the dining room and into the kitchen where her mother sat at the kitchen table, trying to mend a broken porcelain vase with Krazy Glue. There were at least twenty pieces of various sizes laid out on the table.

"What happened, Mom?"

"I knocked it over while I was vacuuming. It had to be one of my favorites, too."

"You don't really think you can fix it, do you?" Sarah asked skeptically.

"I'm going to try."

"But you'll see all the cracks even if you do manage to put it back together."

"Only if you look for them, dear." Mrs. Jordan refused to be discouraged.

Sarah just shrugged and sat down at the table to watch the mending.

"Mom?" she said after a minute or two, "can I talk to you about something?"

"Sure, what is it?"

"When you were in college, you spent your junior year in France, didn't you?"

"Yes. In Paris. It was wonderful." She continued to work on the vase, but her voice was dreamy.

"When you were there, did you ever meet any Belgians?"

"As a matter of fact, I did. I spent a weekend in Brussels once with some relatives of people I had met in Paris."

"What were the Belgians like?"

"How do you mean?"

"Well, do they have any peculiar customs? Are they different from the French?"

"Indeed, they are. The French-speaking Belgians,

at least the ones I met, were very conservative people, very straitlaced. I remember my Parisian friend warning me that Belgians dressed for every meal. And they did."

"Oh. . . ."

"Why are you so interested in Belgians?"

"Well, ah . . . I know someone. . . . There's this boy at school, Mom. He's from Belgium. We get along pretty well, but he's very . . . proper. I want him to loosen up, but he won't. I thought maybe because you lived in Europe. . . ." Sarah let her sentence go unfinished as she realized that she really didn't know what she wanted to ask.

Mrs. Jordan looked up from her vase. "What's your interest in this boy? Or shouldn't I ask?"

"Well, you know. I kind of like him. And I think he likes me. But we're not on the same wavelength, and I'm afraid we never will be." There was a note of despair in Sarah's voice.

"Oh." Mrs. Jordan pursed her lips and glanced down at her work. "What about Steve?"

Sarah sighed deeply and stared at the tabletop. "David didn't tell you?"

"Well, frankly he didn't have to, Sarah. I had an inkling something was about to come to a head between you two."

"You did?" Sarah was genuinely surprised.

"You probably didn't think we noticed, but your father and I could see that you haven't been very happy these past few months. I figured it had to be because of Steve. The way you'd come home every day and rifle through the mail was a dead giveaway. I really felt for you, but I didn't say anything. But to be honest, I had my doubts about how long your relationship would last after he left for college."

"Well, it's all over now. At least I know where things stand, and that's a real relief."

"But do you think it's wise to get involved with someone else so soon? Don't you want to give yourself a little time?"

"Well, truthfully, Mom, I sort of felt—on my own—that it was over between me and Steve, too. And I've got to admit I've had my eye on this other guy since school started—even though I couldn't forget Steve."

"So now you figure you're free to pursue this Belgian?"

"It's not like that, Mom. It's not like I kept him stringing along just in case something happened with Steve."

"No, dear, I didn't mean it that way. I know you're not like that."

"You see, Bernard—that's the Belgian—was at the concert, the one we all went to in New York. We sat together and we had a really great time. He loosened up there and enjoyed himself. Unfortunately he tightened up again afterward. In school he's just so formal and polite he's hard to get close to."

"Sounds as though you really like him." Mrs. Jordan smiled kindly.

"I guess I do. But I think he likes me, too. He's just too bashful or whatever to do anything about it. Sometimes I think I'll have to dye my hair platinum, wear a lot of makeup and carry a sign that says 'Bernard—Come Get Me.'"

"Just the opposite, Sarah."

"What do you mean?"

"From what I remember of the Belgians, coming on strong will scare him off. Most Europeans think that American girls are aggressive anyway. I would imagine you'd have to be subtle with him. In other words, just be yourself, Sarah."

"That's what I've been doing, but it doesn't seem to work."

"I would guess that part of the problem is that he can't bring himself to approach you first. In Belgium people are always formally introduced. They never just meet. But since this isn't Belgium, he probably feels awkward, so you'll have to take the initiative. Maybe you'll be able to break down his inhibitions and something'll happen."

Sarah looked dubious. "I hope it doesn't take forever to melt his inhibitions. The Winter Carnival Ball is just two and a half weeks off."

"Well, play it cool and make sure you see him at least once a day."

"Gee, Mom, I feel a little funny talking about this kind of thing with my own mother."

"Why? I want you to be happy. And from what you've said, I think I'd like this Bernard."

"Yeah, but you never think of your own mother figuring out how to catch a boy."

"Silly, how do you think I got your father to notice me?"

Sarah giggled and blushed at the thought of her parents as teenagers dating.

"There's just one thing that bothers me," Mrs. Jordan murmured as she went back to work on her vase.

"What's that?"

"I don't know how in heaven's name I'm going to glue this thing back together."

Sarah exhaled with relief. "If your advice works, Mom, I'll buy you a new one. Imported from Belgium!"

14

Sarah sat in the cafeteria, casually leafing through a copy of *Seventeen* magazine and picking at her salad. She was waiting for Bernard. Not to eat with him or ask him anything in particular, but just to say hello. That's all. Well, for now at least.

She glanced at the line of kids going through the serving bay, then looked at her watch. Fifteen minutes into fifth period and no sign of him. There's still time. Be cool. Remember what Mom said.

Flipping the pages of her magazine, she came upon a full-page photo of a group of models in khaki skirts and shorts, button-down collar shirts, string ties, and monogramed crew-neck sweaters. Each one wore the exact same pair of tortoiseshell Annie Hall glasses. The caption under the photo was "The

Preppy Look: Spring Semester Fashions." "The enemy," she whispered to herself.

She looked all around the cafeteria, but there was still no Bernard. Where could he be? This is his lunch period. She stared out the window at the passing cars, wondering whether Bernard was worth the effort or whether she would just get hurt in the end. Not going to the Winter Carnival Ball wouldn't be the end of the world, she reasoned. It's the prom that really counts. Of course, there's a good chance that if he takes Lisa to the ball, he'll take her to the prom, too. All of a sudden she was as anxious as ever.

"Excuse me. Is this the Bird Watchers Society?"

"What?" Sarah snapped her head around and saw Penny setting her tray down on the table.

"Oh, it's *you*, Sarah. The way you were gazing out the window, I thought you were a bird watcher."

Not a bird watcher—a Bernard watcher, Sarah thought. "Very funny, Penny. Who writes your material? Miss Edwards?"

"No, I hear she keeps all her material for herself."

"Maybe you should book her for your Junior Professionals' Theater."

"What a great idea, Sarah! I think I'll suggest that. We can bill her as the Faerie Queene of Comedy."

"Yeah! Then maybe you could send her out on the road with her act. That way English would be canceled for the year!"

"Dream on!"

Sarah glanced at her watch again and looked over at the lunch line.

"Speaking of acts, Sarah, how's your recital coming along?"

"It's really shaping up pretty well. To my great surprise."

"Why do you say that?"

"Well, these kids from Jefferson who take lessons from us have only been playing instruments for a couple of months now. No one ever thought they would have been able to play decent scales this soon. But Jon has been a real incentive for them. Not only does he encourage each one of them individually, now he's arranging pieces for them to play at the recital. You know, stuff that's on their level but still sounds okay. He's really remarkable." Sarah craned her neck to look over Penny's head at the serving bay again.

"What's your kid going to play?" Penny asked.

"Joey? He's getting his big wish. Jon has organized two rock groups out of the pupils, and Joey is in one of them. Joey's group is doing 'Stayin' Alive,' the other group is doing 'Free Bird.' And they both sound pretty good."

"Have you decided what you're going to do for the recital yet?"

"Believe it or not, I may be playing a duet with Naomi after all. She's getting an arrangement of 'America' from *West Side Story* for two pianos. If it's as easy as she says it is, we'll do it."

"I hope you do. It's my favorite number from that show."

Sarah turned all the way around and scoured the room with her gaze.

"Are you by any chance waiting for someone?" Penny asked.

"Who? Me? No."

"Then why are you looking all over the place like that? You've been doing it ever since I sat down."

"Just bird watching," Sarah sighed, "that's all." She speared a slice of cucumber from her salad, examined it for a moment, then dropped it back into her dish.

Bernard never showed up at the cafeteria, and Sarah spent the entire sixth period worrying about it. How am I supposed to run into him if I can't find him? This'll never work. There's not enough time for subtle tactics. It may be too late already.

All through her sixth-period homeroom, she pondered her situation and fretted over Bernard. Eventually her head was filled with new schemes and ideas, anything just to get close to Bernard. As she racked her brain for the perfect plan, she doodled in her notebook, drawing musical notes, guitars, interlocking cubes, Bs, and arrows all over the page.

Maybe Lisa has the right idea. Come on like gangbusters and he can't ignore you. But the thought of playing on Lisa's level was distasteful to her. Better to stay home and miss all the fun than to start acting like Lisa, she decided.

Sarah's chain of thought was broken when she dropped her pen on the floor. She bent down automatically to pick it up, but then it came to her. Gazing at her pen on the floor, she grinned mischievously. It's corny, but it might work. Can't hurt to try.

She picked up her pen and put it in her bag, then looked at her watch. It was ten to one. One hour till Ms. Stillman's class. I'll see him there for sure.

Sarah rushed so that she would be early for her last period class. When she got to Ms. Stillman's class, there were only a few people seated and Bernard hadn't arrived yet.

She glanced furtively around the room, focusing on the fourth seat from the front in the row by the windows, Bernard's usual place.

Setting her books down in her usual seat—the third desk in the second row from the door—Sarah pondered just how she was going to pull this off and make it look natural. She walked to a window and stared out, still not exactly sure what she would do. She started to have second thoughts.

But then Bernard walked into the classroom, lugging his gym bag over his shoulder. Just coming from the showers, his hair was still wet at the ends and his complexion was ruddy. He looked straight at Sarah and smiled.

Something gripped her stomach in that instant and her knees got a little wobbly.

He walked right up to her. "Hello, Sarah. How are you today?"

"Oh, fine. And you?"

"Good, very good." He seemed more friendly than usual. She hadn't planned on his helping out.

"Say, Bernard . . ."

"Yes, Sarah?" He smiled warmly.

"Do you have a pen I can borrow? I must have lost mine."

"Yes, of course." He reached into his jacket pocket and came up with a Bic ball-point. "Will this do?"

"Thanks. I'll give it back to you after class."

"No problem." He was still smiling, not his usual serious self.

Ms. Stillman swept in, calling the class to order. Kids shuffled to their seats, and a flurry of murmurs and giggles quickly came and went as the teacher started to lecture.

Sarah took her seat, clutching Bernard's pen. *Now for step two*, she thought, a little bit nervous.

Step two was a breeze. As soon as the bell rang and Ms. Stillman had dismissed the class, Sarah dashed out of the room and headed for her locker. All she had to do was kill some time until 3:45 when Bernard would be finishing up his guitar lesson. If she "just happened" to be up by the music school at 3:45 when he gave his lesson, she could return his pen. She grinned mischievously. It would be easy.

Unfortunately, it wasn't that easy. After lingering over a soda at Burger King while doing her math homework, Sarah went back to school. The hallways were eerily silent, but she felt more at ease knowing that no one else was around. Returning Bernard's pen like this was still a ploy, and having thought about it, she wasn't exactly proud of herself for going through with it. It was so manipulative, not like her at all. She kept telling herself it was only a means to an end, however, a happy end.

But when she finally reached the fourth floor, her heart sank. The door to the music room was closed, and several people were gathered outside, including Gary and some of the other music teachers. And Lisa Forster and two of her friends. The guys were nodding and grinning, listening intently by the door, while Lisa and her girl friends were whispering, huddled together by the wall opposite the music room.

Sarah wanted to scream. She wanted to run downstairs and out of the building she felt so foolish. What if someone asks what I'm doing here at quarter to four? Returning a stupid pen to Bernard? This is retarded! I'm retarded!

She hoped no one would notice her standing at the end of the hall, but Gary had already spotted her. He waved her over, swinging his long, skinny arms. There was nothing else she could do now. She had to go over and see what was happening.

"Hey, Sarah," Gary whispered as she approached, "come here and listen to this." He pointed to the door.

Then she heard it. Guitars—a guitar duet. She listened for a minute. It was a beautiful, tender ballad. A series of bittersweet jazz chords providing a framework for an intense, interlaced, classical-style lead.

Burning with curiosity, she peeked through the window in the door and saw that it was Bernard and

Jon. They were sitting in front of a single music stand, both focused on the music before them. Jon's face seemed uncustomarily serious as he strummed the complex chord progressions, keeping the rhythm. Bernard's brow was furrowed as he bent over his guitar. She couldn't see his hands, but his fingers must have been working furiously from what Sarah could hear. It was such an oddly enchanting melody—half-jazz, half-baroque, but completely unique. The piece didn't have the kind of catchy melody you could hum, but Sarah knew she wouldn't forget it.

"Is this too much or what?" Gary whispered enthusiastically.

"They're great! Both of them!" Jimmy Nobile cut in. "They should record it."

"What is it?" Sarah asked.

"It's something Bernard wrote," Gary replied. "He and Jon are gonna play it for the recital next week."

"It really is unusual. I don't think I've ever heard anything quite like it."

"But don't you think it's great?" Jimmy's eyes were wide with excitement.

"Yes, it's absolutely wonderful," she agreed. "But what are *they* doing here?" She nodded toward Lisa and the preppies across the hall.

"Who knows?" Gary shrugged. "They just showed up. They never talk to me, thank heavens."

Sarah looked over at Lisa and caught her eye. Lisa smiled slyly and waved. Sarah went over to her, still feeling angry and resentful.

"Hi, Lisa," she whispered coolly, "what brings *you* up here?"

"Bernard. What else?"

"Oh?" Sarah wanted to slap her so much it hurt.

"Yes, of course." Lisa then leaned forward as if about to share a secret with Sarah. "He doesn't know it yet, but he's taking me to the Winter Carnival Ball."

"Uh-huh." Sarah was seeing red. It was a struggle not to blow her cool.

"What brings *you* up here?" Lisa asked as if Sarah was trespassing.

"Me? I . . . ah, wanted to use the piano. To rehearse for the recital. But it looks as though they'll be in there for a while," she nodded toward the music room.

"Oh, I suspect they will. After all, this will be the featured number of the recital."

"Really? I didn't hear anything about any featured number." Sarah's heart was pounding furiously.

"Well, of course. Bernard is the best musician in the school. After all, would Jon Pearce have chosen Bernie to play a duet with him if he weren't a star performer?"

"Well, it doesn't look as though I'll get in there today, so I guess I'll shove off. Bye." She turned on her heel like a cadet and marched down the hall.

"Bye, Sarah."

Lisa's singsong voice was infuriating. Nevertheless, Sarah looked straight ahead and trod down the hall, trying to control the fury boiling inside her. Her

168

steps echoed in the stairwell like a taut snare drum's beat. But then she couldn't hold it in any longer. On the third-floor landing, the tears began to stream down her hot cheeks.

That witch! That awful—! Who does she think she is! And why does she think anyone would want to go anywhere with her?

Scheming. Plotting. Planning. It stinks, it all stinks! Why did I ever think this stupid business with the pen would work? Why did I think I could out-Lisa Lisa? It serves me right! Serves me right for descending to her level! How could I be so dumb? It serves me right!

Pushing through the main door's crash bars, she ran out of the building at full tilt. Her hands trembling, she stopped abruptly at the bottom of the front steps and fumbled into the side pouch of her bag. Finding the object of her former hopes, she flung Bernard's pen into the bushes.

15

I'll be a spinster piano teacher if I have to, she kept telling herself after that awful Thursday afternoon. Chasing boys stinks! It only makes you miserable. Better that I do something creative with my time instead of hunting for shy Belgians, like Lisa Forster. It's my music that really matters, she decided.

She was true to her vow, practicing her number for the recital with a vengeance. In fact, she and Naomi were so impressive at the dress rehearsal, Jon decided that they should open the show. And sitting at the piano on the night of the recital, Sarah even impressed herself. A week ago she never would have thought she'd have been able to keep up with Naomi, but tonight she was doing much more than just keeping up. The Latin rhythm of "America" was infectious enough, but performing it in front of an audience was a real high. As they stepped up the beat and modulated to the next key, the excitement mounted and Sarah could almost see the leaping dancers and swirling skirts from the movie version of *West Side Story*. "La-la-la-la in Amer-ee-ca. . . ." The words shouted in her head as she played, a grin creeping onto her face despite her previous week of self-imposed absolute seriousness.

She glanced over at Naomi at her piano. Unlike her usually stern performance demeanor, Naomi's face was a portrait of bliss.

She deserves it, Sarah thought, more convinced than ever that she had done the right thing in concentrating on her music and trying to forget about Bernard. Even if she wasn't doing such a good job of forgetting him, she knew she was instrumental in making at least two people happy, Naomi and Joey Blake. When she wasn't rehearsing with Naomi, Sarah was coaching Joey Blake, who was delirious about being part of an honest-to-goodness rock group.

Sarah and Naomi finished "America" with a barrage of staccato chords. The audience loved it, applauding wildly, some even whistling and shouting their approval. The girls took their bows, but Sarah's mind was on Joey now. His rock group, the Mumps, was playing on this half of the program, and she felt she should be with him just in case he needed her. All week she had doted over him, giving him point-ers and advice. Of course, Joey had no way of knowing that Sarah's attentiveness at least partially stemmed from her desire to avoid Bernard. Everyone had to be at group rehearsals for the recital, but Sarah figured Bernard would not interrupt her if she were involved with Joey and the Mumps.

And she was right. Bernard did not apprach her at all. Their relationship consisted of fleeting "hi's" in the hallway and tentative nods in History class. Sarah figured Bernard didn't know what was really going on with her because he remained cordial and friendly whenever they met. She felt it was better that way. No telling what a gallant Belgian might do if he suspected he had hurt her, and Sarah wasn't interested in sympathy from anyone, including him.

As hard as she tried, though, she could not drive from her mind the thought of Lisa and Bernard together. It just isn't right, she'd reasoned as she stared across the auditorium at him during rehearsals. He deserves better. But why in the world doesn't he realize that? Do all guys just automatically fall for these pushy girls? Like Steve's college girl no doubt. Doesn't anyone want a nice, normal girl anymore? These angry questions obsessed her so much all week long that it never occurred to her that she hadn't heard Bernard rehearsing anything for the recital. He and Jon hadn't performed their duet at any of the rehearsals, but Sarah had been completely oblivious to that.

The curtain closed, and Naomi gave Sarah an unexpected hug. "We were great, Sarah! We were great!"

"Yes . . . I'm speechless. Come on, Naomi. Let's get off stage. We're just in the way here."

Standing in the wings was Ms. Stillman, looking very happy. "Very nice, girls. You were terrific. I think you really broke the ice."

"Thanks, Ms. Stillman."

"Yeah, thanks." Sarah was still searching all around her. *He's someplace backstage,* she thought. *I better find Joey.*

Distractedly she wandered away from Naomi and Ms. Stillman and wound her way through the wings, up the back stairs, and into the first-floor hallway where the upcoming performers waited for their curtain. She spotted Joey immediately; his satiny blood-red shirt was impossible to miss. He was leaning against the wall, one foot propped up behind him, his arms folded over his chest, talking to the other Mumps.

"Hi, Joey. How do you feel? Are you nervous?" Sarah descended upon him like a mother hen.

"No problem, Sarah. Don't sweat it." He was as cocky as ever. "I'll be great."

"Don't count on it. You haven't been in front of a real audience yet. Now when you get out there—"

"Take it easy, will ya? It'll be cool."

"Ha!" Barbara, the Mumps' drummer, cut in.

"Whadd'ya mean 'ha'?" Joey was on the defensive.

"Who do you think you're kidding, Joey? You're just as nervous as the rest of us."

"Speak for yourself."

173

"Come on, Joey. I know all the places in 'Stayin' Alive' where you always flub it. You can't fool your drummer."

"You're crazy. I know that song backward and forward and inside out, too."

"Oh, yeah?" Barbara stood right up next to him. Although they were the same age, she was a head taller than him.

"Yeah? What're you gonna do about it?"

"All right, you two. Enough!" Sarah intervened. "Listen, if you go on stage with hard feelings like this, they'll throw rotten tomatoes at you. You'll sound awful unless you make up right now. Joey, apologize to Barbara."

"Why? She started it."

"I did not—"

"All right, suit yourselves. I won't bother me one bit if you make fools of yourselves. Heavens, I thought everybody knew that enemies can't make music together."

"The Mumps are on next," a disembodied voice came from the end of the corridor. "Two minutes to curtain."

Joey sighed. Now he looked worried. "You sure you're not just jivin' us about this, Sarah?"

"Would I lie to you?"

"Okay, okay. Barbara, I apologize. Are we friends?" He held out his hand and looked begrudgingly contrite.

Barbara took his hand eagerly. "Friends," she confirmed.

"Okay, guys." Joey's humility was brief. "Let's go. Don't want to be late for my . . . er, *our* debut."

The Mumps shuffled off down the hall, a motley little crew made up of two shaggy-haired guitarists, a chubby bass player, their very tall young lady drummer, and Sarah's "little Mozart." She smiled proudly at them. *He's a pain in the neck,* she thought, *but he's all mine.*

Anxious to see the historic first performance of the Mumps, Sarah ran down the front stairs to the auditorium entrance. She stood up in the back to watch. The Mumps were all plugged in and ready to go. Barbara clicked her drumsticks together for the downbeat, then they tore into "Stayin' Alive" like rock munchkins. True, they were still ragged and a bit sloppy, but for kids who had only been playing instruments for a few months, they could have been considered prodigies. And the fact that the two guitarists' voices hadn't changed yet made it all the better because they sounded exactly like the Bee Gees' falsettos on the original version of "Stayin' Alive." Joey didn't sing, of course, because his voice was too bizarre. But it didn't seem to matter from the ecstatic look on his face. Sarah was moved by his joyous expression as he bobbed up and down to the beat. She was very happy that she had spent the past week rehearsing every afternoon with Joey and Naomi.

The last act of the first half of the recital was a baroque brass trio—Christopher Barry and Joseph Lemire on trumpets and Walter Latimore on trombone. They were pretty good, a soothing, majestic blend, the perfect ending for the first half of the show, Sarah felt.

At intermission, Sarah scoured the audience, looking for Penny. She found her on her way to the Ladies' Room. Penny said she was very impressed with Sarah's number and congratulated her profusely. But Penny was also full of hot gossip, as usual, and on their way back to the auditorium, she shared the latest rumor with her friend.

"Sarah, have you heard the latest about Jon Pearce and Kathy Stillman?"

"No, what?"

"They're getting very tight, I hear. Maybe even thinking about getting married," Penny whispered.

"Ms. Stillman and Jon? Are you sure?"

"That's what I heard?"

"From Gary."

"Gary?" Sarah laughed. "Who told Gary?"

"Gary told me he saw them holding hands and sneaking kisses after the recital rehearsals when they thought everyone was gone."

"What was he doing there? Spying for Gossip Central?" Sarah jerked her thumb at Penny.

"He said he was packing up his drums. And I know for a fact that it takes forever to pack those things."

"Well, I don't know what he saw, but I'm still skeptical."

But then Sarah remembered the mortgage Jon was getting through her father's bank. Maybe he had been thinking about settling down when he bought the house. They had seemed pretty tight in the bus on the way to the Billy Joel/Makers concert. Could they already have been making plans back then?

She decided not to mention Jon's house to Penny, unwilling to add circumstantial evidence to the rumor. Anyway she'd promised her father a long time ago that she wouldn't tell anyone about it.

"Well, anyway," Penny fluttered her hand as if to brush the rumor off, "I just thought I'd tell you in case it turned out to be true."

"So how do you like the recital so far?"

"Not bad, not bad at all. I don't know what you did to Naomi, but it definitely is an improvement."

"Naomi's good people when you give her a chance. But frankly until we started rehearsing 'America,' I didn't think she could play anything written after 1900."

"Yeah, but she isn't half the drip we thought she was," Penny admitted with a half-smile. "I guess I'll have to stop making fun of her."

"Awfully generous of you, my dear," Sarah complimented in a British accent.

"Oh, don't mention it, your majesty," she replied in kind.

"And how about the rest of the show? What did you think of the Mumps?"

"Now they were a real stitch. They reminded me of disco chipmunks. And Joey! He must have thought he was John Travolta or something, the way he was bopping behind his piano."

"Oh, no. He'd tell you he was *better* than Travolta if you asked him to get up and dance."

"My only complaint so far is with the audience. The preppy queen and her court to be exact. They're awful! Talking out loud during the performances, combing their hair. And Lisa is the worst, of course. She looks like a real campus cutie tonight. And you can guess whom she's dressed up for."

Sarah certainly could guess, but she wasn't going to think about that. Not after spending the past week trying to forget him. She felt that even simply mentioning his name could be dangerous, like a magic word that would unlock a cave full of unhappiness. No, this topic had to be dropped because it would surely lead to another sore subject—the purpose of Lisa Forster's inexhaustible efforts to snare Bernard, the Winter Carnival Ball. Sarah didn't want to know if they were going together. She told herself she didn't care. Having resigned herself to the fact that she was not going, Sarah wasn't interested in hearing anything else about the ball. Or so she kept telling herself.

By now they were back at Penny's seat and the houselights were flashing on and off, signaling the start of the second part of the recital.

"I have to go, Penny. I'd sit with you, but I have to wait backstage for the curtain call," Sarah said quickly. "Maybe I'll see you after the show."

"Okay. Bye."

Sarah slipped through the doorway that led backstage, still wary of running into Bernard. She wanted to see the rest of the show, but she really wasn't in the mood for chitchat or backstage horseplay. Then she got an idea.

178

The stage was constructed oddly with all the backstage dressing rooms on stage-left and only a small space big enough for three or four people in the stage-right wings. It was the perfect place to hang out for the rest of the show, she thought. There were even a couple of folding chairs over there. With less than a minute to go before the next act went on, Sarah calmly walked across the stage, trying not to look conspicuous, and nestled herself into the stage-right cubbyhole.

She stayed there for the rest of the show. No one seemed to miss her, and she felt quite secure watching the show from her own secluded vantage point. But when the last number of the show was announced, her anxieties began to grow again. She started to fantasize about all the awful possibilities that existed beyond her safe little cubbyhole. Bernard could try to start up a conversation with her after the show. Then Lisa could show up. *If I could only stay here until everyone went home,* she thought.

Her ruminations were suddenly disturbed. Without her noticing it, someone had crept up behind the backdrop curtain against the wall behind the stage and was now in the corner, hidden in the shadows just a few feet from Sarah. Instantly Sarah felt imposed upon; her private space had been invaded.

Quietly she turned in her seat and peered into the dark corner, where a tall figure stood facing the wall. Who is it? What is he doing?

Gary's rock group was on stage, ripping through a searing version of Chuck Berry's "Johnny B.

Goode." Sarah wasn't paying attention to them, though. Her eyes were riveted to the dark figure in the corner. Then the kid working the lights shifted the direction of a followspot and a sliver of white light slipped into the dark corner illuminating it just enough for Sarah to make out who the intruder was.

It wasn't one person, it was two. The tall one was Jon Pearce, the other one behind him was Kathy Stillman. Sarah saw them locked in a tender embrace, their lips pressed together.

Penny was right, she realized. Then she wished she could shrink to about mouse-size so she could creep away unnoticed. *If they see me, I'll just die right here,* she thought. She turned around slowly, careful not to make a sound, and stared intently at the band on stage. If they see me watching the band like this, maybe they'll think I didn't see them.

Sarah didn't budge until the band was finished and she could see Ms. Stillman and Jon on the other side of the stage, standing in the wings. They seemed to be looking for someone. Jon was holding his acoustic guitar, looking concerned. Finally Sarah saw Jon and Kathy Stillman shrug to each other. Then Bernard came up behind Jon. He was holding his guitar, too. The three of them exchanged a few words, Bernard and Jon shaking their heads as if in disappointment, then Ms. Stillman went out on stage.

"We'd like to thank you all for coming tonight, ladies and gentlemen," she announced to the crowd. "But please don't leave yet because we have a special treat in store for you—an original piece composed by one of our music teachers, Bernard St.

180

Onge. And it will be performed by Mr. St. Onge and Mr. Jon Pearce."

The crowd gasped. Jon Pearce himself was going to play! The momentarily hushed audience exploded into applause when the curtain opened, revealing Jon and Bernard seated together on stools, their guitars poised on their laps. The applause would have just gone on and on if Jon hadn't raised one hand, calling for silence.

"Thank you," he said, getting the crowd's attention. "As Kathy told you, we are going to play a piece written by Bernard especially for tonight." Bernard nodded shyly at the mention of his name. "It's called 'Serenade to Sarah.'"

What! What did he say? Serenade to Sarah? Sarah's heart started to beat faster, her breath got a little shorter, her face was hot and flushed.

She gazed out at the stage where two single spotlights cast long shadows across the stage. They started to play, and Sarah recognized it immediately. It was that song, the one they had been playing in the music room that afternoon, that horrible afternoon. The bittersweet chords and intricate spritely melody was very familiar to her, only it was even better now, richer, with more complicated counterpoint, and a lot more feeling. The music filled her ears and caressed her. The guitar strains seemed to be wafting straight toward her, like a personal radio broadcast in the middle of the night.

But it couldn't be for. . . . No, he must know another Sarah. His sister maybe, she thought.

But he didn't have any sisters. She had to consider

the obvious and wonderful probability that she was the one.

The song ran its magical course, mesmerizing the audience. Then thunderous applause and happy confusion backstage after the curtain closed.

Dizzy, light-headed, in love, Sarah remained tucked away in her secret hiding place.

16

When someone writes a song for you, then gets up to play it in front of hundreds of people, it must mean something. Right? she thought.

She had to find out, one way or the other, but she was still reluctant to leave her hiding place in the wings.

If only I didn't have to see all those other people first. If I could just find Bernard, just to make sure!

But she knew that sneaking out was impossible. If she left through the stage and walked into the audience, someone was sure to stop her and ask her about that song. Penny would be the first to find her; she was like a homing pigeon when there was hot gossip in the air. But that was fine with Sarah. Better to have Penny around for support, especially when you knew the preppy queen was also lurking in the crowd.

Lisa Forster was the one person in the whole world that Sarah had to avoid at all cost. After all the bragging she had done about how she was going to have Bernard, Lisa was surely livid now.

But I can't hide here forever! This is silly, she thought.

Then she thought of something else—Jon and Ms. Stillman kissing behind the backdrop curtain.

If I'm very careful, I can sneak behind that curtain. When the coast is clear on the other side, I can run to the back stairway where the coatrack is, grab my coat, and keep going right out to the parking lot. That's it!

The only thing she thought about now was getting out unseen. She'd worry about everything else later, including explaining to Penny and her parents why she had disappeared after the recital when she had promised to meet them afterward. Her heart was pounding in her ears as she tiptoed through the narrow space behind the backdrop curtain, making sure she didn't rustle it and give her position away.

When she got to the other side, she peered out very carefully. The coast seemed to be clear, only a few of the Jefferson kids were still around and they wouldn't bother her. Sarah took a deep breath, put her head down, and walked quickly toward the back stairwell.

All went well until she got to the coatrack. Turning the corner, she saw someone down there, shrugging into her coat. Sarah froze, hoping whoever this was wouldn't notice her.

Having buttoned her coat, the shadowy figure proceeded to the back door that led to the parking lot, but before she pushed the crash bar, she turned around and looked right up at Sarah. It was Ms. Stillman.

"Sarah!" she called out in a pleasant but surprised voice. "Where've you been? We've been looking for you."

"Oh . . . I was watching the show," Sarah's voice betrayed her intention to be evasive in her answers.

"We looked all over for you. You weren't in the audience." Kathy Stillman seemed extra friendly in an oddly coaxing way. She smiled warmly at Sarah as if she were trying to reassure her of something.

"I was by myself. In the wings on the other side of the stage."

Ms. Stillman's eyes widened, then a mischievous grin spread across her face. "How long were you there?"

"The whole second half of the show."

"I see." Ms. Stillman giggled and blushed. "How did you like the . . . show?"

"The show? Oh, it was great, very nice." Now Sarah was smiling broadly. It was clear that they were on to each other.

"You know, Sarah, Bernard has been looking all over for you."

"He has?" Sarah's heart leapt.

"Uh-huh."

"Where is he now?"

"I don't know. I hope he didn't go home." Ms. Stillman was still grinning.

185

"Gee, I hope not, too."

"Well, if I see him, should I let him know you're looking for him?"

"Ah, yeah. Please do."

"Okay. See you on Monday, Sarah."

"Bye."

Sarah was frantic and crazy and delighted. She leapt down the stairs like an Olympic gymnast, threw on her coat and burst through the back doors. The night was starless and cold. Floodlights perched over the parking lot made the groups of people going to their cars look like walking silhouettes with misty clouds of breath coming from their shadowy heads.

He must be out here someplace. . . . But where? she wondered.

She was afraid he might leave without seeing her, and this couldn't wait till Monday. Haphazardly she darted through the parking lot, looking for a muscular silhouette carrying a guitar case.

But then she found the next best thing—the St. Onges' metallic blue Peugeot station wagon, the car that had picked up Bernard after the Billy Joel/Makers concert. She was sure it was the right car because there was a faculty parking sticker from the university on the driver's vent window. He had to come come back to the car, she figured. If she just waited here, she couldn't miss Bernard and his parents.

Leaning on the cold fender of the Peugeot, she waited, watching other cars leave but turning away from the glare of passing headlights. After fifteen minutes, there were only a few cars left in the lot. But still no Bernard.

Then she heard that back door open and slam shut. The sound of boots on pavement preceded a dark figure carrying a guitar case. Sarah became light-headed and nervous. The dark stranger approached her, but she could only see a shadow because the bright floodlights were shining in her eyes. Then the approaching figure stepped forward and blocked out the glaring light, and suddenly she could see him perfectly. It was Bernard!

"Sarah!" He seemed startled. "I've . . . been looking for you."

"I know. Ms. Stillman told me."

"Oh. Well, I just wanted to ask you . . . if you like my 'Serenade.'"

"Yes, I loved it." She gulped. "The title. Is it for—?"

"Yes, Sarah"—he coughed nervously and looked at the ground for a moment—"it is dedicated to you." He gazed into her eyes. "I wrote it for you," he repeated in his full voice, with a tender, hopeful smile. He took her hand and squeezed it.

"Thank you . . ." she could barely whisper.

"I like you very much, Sarah. But I could not be like American boys, so bold. I did not know how else to tell you how I felt."

Speechless with joy, she hugged him tightly, and as he brought his strong arms around her, his lips found hers. They kissed tenderly, lovingly. It was so wonderful, Sarah hoped it would never end.

Finally, after what seemed like a very long time, he pulled away gently. "Sarah," he whispered, "will you go to the Winter Carnival Ball with me?"

Happy tears brimmed in her eyes. "I'd love to, yes," she breathed into his ear.

In the empty parking lot of Maplewood High, the floodlights were on Sarah and Bernard as they kissed, their love warming them against the chilly December night.

If you enjoyed this book...

...you will enjoy a *First Love* from Silhouette subscription even more. It will bring you each new title, as soon as it is published every month, delivered right to your door.

Filled with the challenges, excitement and anticipation that make first love oh, so wonderful, *First Love* romances are new and different. Every *First Love* romance is an original novel—never before published—and all written by leading authors.

If you enjoyed this book, treat yourself, or some friend, to a one-year subscription to these romantic originals. We'll ship two NEW $1.75 romances each month, a total of 24 books a year. So send in your coupon now. **There's nothing quite as special as a First Love.**

First Love from Silhouette

NEW BOY IN TOWN
Sixteen-year-old Stacey Hippner loves her parents but she resents their restrictions—especially when they involve Garr Garwin, the new boy in town.

KATE HERSELF
Kate Fleming had always felt the insignificant middle sister. That was before Ross Barrow, the most popular boy in school asked her out.

PLEASE LET ME IN
Melissa Johnson had always dreamed of being in with the most popular crowd. When Greg Scott, hero of the high school football team, begins to date her, she feels she has really made it.

FLOWERS FOR LISA
Lisa Kelly's interest in flowers earns her a summer job at Rick Brewster's father's florist shop. She is thrilled when she and Rick start dating. But she wonders if their relationship will turn out to be only a summer romance.

GIRL IN THE ROUGH
Kate's life as the brainy big sister of adorable, popular Mimi was not easy. When Kate took up golf all this changed.

First Love from Silhouette

THERE'S NOTHING QUITE AS SPECIAL AS A <u>FIRST LOVE</u>.

_____ #1 **NEW BOY IN TOWN** $1.75
       Dorothy Francis

_____ #2 **GIRL IN THE ROUGH** $1.75
       Josephine Wunsch

_____ #3 **PLEASE LET ME IN** $1.75
       Patti Beckman

_____ #4 **SERENADE** $1.75
       Adrienne Marceau

_____ #5 **FLOWERS FOR LISA** $1.75
       Veronica Ladd

_____ #6 **KATE HERSELF** $1.75
       Helen Erskine

First Love from Silhouette

Look for These
New First Love Romances from
Silhouette Books Next Month

Songbird

Carrie Enfield

Tammy Hastings had never felt that she was especially good at anything. That was before Jeff Berger had asked her to sing with him on Talent Night. Overnight she became a star! Soon Jeff became the center of her life. But she had to learn that you can't always command love— sometimes you just have to let it happen....

Special Girl

Dorothy Francis

There was something special between them, Pete Karmer told Vonnie Morrison. And that made moving to a new town easier. This time Vonnie was determined to be outgoing and friendly. But her determination to hide a part of her life caused misunderstandings and, worse yet, threatened to break up her first real romance.